T0156760

THE OMEGA PROJECT

THE OMEGA PROJECT

*The Spectacular End
to a Cruel Dictatorship*

By

Byron Daring

iUniverse, Inc.
Bloomington

The Omega Project
The Spectacular End to a Cruel Dictatorship

iUniverse books may be ordered through booksellers or by contacting:

iUniverse
1663 Liberty Drive
Bloomington, IN 47403
www.iuniverse.com
1-800-Authors (1-800-288-4677)

ISBN: 978-1-4759-6589-6 (sc)
ISBN: 978-1-4759-6590-2 (ebk)

Library of Congress Control Number: 2012923073

Printed in the United States of America

iUniverse rev. date: 12/17/2012

TABLE OF CONTENTS

SYNOPSIS

The author has developed a plot, which succeeds in eliminating a dictator while sparing the lives of innocent people. The motivation to write this book stemmed from the failure to terminate a long lasting dictatorship. It offers a modus operandi to eliminate dictatorships wherever they develop.

The book describes a realistic mechanism to depose a dictator and presents a plausible scenario that could follow this termination.

THE FRUITLESS EFFORTS TO END THE ISLA GRANDE DICTATORSHIP

Many efforts to end dictatorships have failed. They have included international public opinion, as expressed in newspapers, television reports, radio programs, movies, etc. The United Nations, and other international organizations such as the Organization of American States, and human rights groups all over the world, have denounced the tragedy of dictatorship in an effort to make drastic changes, most often unsuccessfully.

Many revolutionary attempts that have not received outside help in assassination efforts have failed. Let us now take you through a hypothetical, but realistic, series of events, which evinces the potential of advances in technology, designed by man to restrain and punish those who break the law.

FOREWORD

No matter when, where, or to whom, we have a responsibility for mankind and our environment. From the beginning of time, man has struggled for survival; first, from the threats of his environment, and later, from others of his own species. Planet Water (Planet Earth) offers wonderful opportunities for the survival of the human race.

At any given time in our history, people have killed each other, not just for protection, but often to impose one's will upon others.

There are countless examples of man's effort to survive. This book is dedicated to the following: those who succeeded; those who lie in silent tombs, sometimes in the vast oceans of our planet, after attempting futile escapes; as well as those who lost their lives in their beloved country fighting for democracy and for the restoration of human rights.

CHAPTER 1

SMALL VESSEL FLOATING ON BISCAYNE BAY

The Florida Keys are a haven for fishermen all year round except for hurricane season which starts June 1 and ends on November 15.

There is a monotonous appearance of the mangroves throughout all the Keys. One can observe small and large areas crossed by inlets which follow a tortuous course. When viewed from the sky, one can observe the crystal clear waters spotted by large rock formations. There is an extensive coral reef which is close to 50 miles long paralleling North Key Largo, which is the largest Key south of Miami. One wonders just how much life there is in these mangroves. There are crocodiles that surface and sometimes walk inland following storms or during the hurricane season.

The waters are filled with fishes. It is not permitted to do spear fishing in the John Pennekamp Coral Park. On low tides, one can see some rocks surfacing. Proper charts are required to course safely, paralleling the east coast of the Florida Keys.

From Key Largo to the first islands of the Bahamas (Bimini) it is only 52 miles. Rafters that venture across the Florida Straits often land in the Florida Keys. This part of Florida is quite popular for skin-diving and fishing. There is a large private club in North Key Largo, which is as large as Key West. This is often a stop for fueling and for the members who, at just one hour from Miami, can enjoy all the amenities of a unique development.

On a Sunday morning, a 52 foot Bertram yacht was cruising the northern part of the Florida Keys along Key Largo. The captain of the vessel was Ramon Gonzalez, a 62-year-old, tanned, handsome, well-built man with tender-looking eyes. The crew consisted of Johnny, a skinny 20-year-old dynamic youngster with inquisitive eyes, and Annie, a 13-year-old slender girl with long blonde hair, a quiet disposition, and a curious expression.

At a distance they were surprised to see an unmanned, fragile-looking, old wooden boat. Ramon asked Johnny to slow down. They looked around for people. Ramon used binoculars to scan the nearby beach. No one was found.

Annie asked her grandfather, "Aby (nickname for grandfather), what are your thoughts about this small boat floating without passengers?

Ramon: "My thoughts go back in time."

Annie: "Will you please tell us more about your thoughts?"

Ramon: The story that I will tell you has a lot to do with us and explains why we are here today. "Let's anchor, move to the cabin and have some cold lemonade."

They moved into the cabin. Johnny and Annie sat in front of Ramon, anxiously waiting for the story that was unveiled.

Ramon said, "Once upon a time in Isla Grande, I lived with your grandmother, in a comfortable large home that I inherited from my father upon his death. I was the administrator of two sugar mills. The export of sugar was the primary industry of Isla Grande. We had a daughter, Lidia, your mother, who was born and raised in the village where I worked.

A couple, who were our neighbors, had a son, Alex, who was about eight years old when his parents died in a terrible automobile accident. We decided to "adopt" him because he had no close relatives. This boy excelled at school and became a physician. He studied in the medical school located in the capital of Isla Grande.

Alex married a lovely lady, Lucia Robles, who had a superb education in France and was the sister of a lawyer who assumed the leadership of a revolution which deposed a dictator who was in power. Isla Grande was suffering from a series of corrupt governments. The lawyer, who became a leader of the student body of the university, was Fito Robles. Disappointingly, Alex and his wife became disenchanted with Fito, the new dictator who took over the government, and with his regime.

After several months in power, Fito became aware of his sister's disagreement, which was embarrassing to him and potentially dangerous because of her popularity and education. Fito ordered her elimination, which occurred by poisoning. Alex had to quit his medical practice and left the island with the pretext of attending a medical meeting abroad. He eventually settled in Miami.

As I will tell you a little later, Alex became the "brain" behind a plot designed to topple Fito's government. He wanted revenge for the killing of his wife. This was a scar on his soul which motivated his future actions. Thanks to him, your grandmother and I were able to come to the United States."

3

Ramon sat comfortably on his fishing seat and began to tell Annie and Johnny the story about a similar small vessel which had the name Cucaracha (which means cockroach).

Ramon looked at Annie, who did not appear bored by his long dissertation. She expressed great interest in continuing to listen to her grandfather.

"Surprisingly to Alex, Lucia, his wife, became disenchanted with her brother, Fito, quite soon before the revolution started. She disagreed with his methods of imposing his ideas. He had ignored his family (mother, brothers and sisters) and became surrounded by communists of the existing Communist Party, as well as by many youngsters who had no military experience but appeared to be idealists.

Every day there were fights in small and large cities where many civilians were killed as collateral damage and this occurred for a period of two to three years.

Finally, after many scrimmages and fights which started in the eastern part of the island and extended to all provinces, Fito arrived triumphantly at the capital on a New Year's Eve. President Matista fled and eventually died in exile.

Annie, many books and movies have been produced as a result of the revolution which had a different outcome than initially expected."

Ramon continued, "There was a great deal of happiness and many expected that the newly constituted government would soon call for elections and that the war would be over. I witnessed many Islanders dressed in uniforms. Many never fought a single battle but were opportunists who joined the rebel forces with the expectations of obtaining a position in the new government.

Fito had promised peace from thereon and asked every citizen of the country to turn in their weapons. He even had a crucifix hanging around his neck, trying to symbolize a religious component to his revolution.

Your grandmother was so fond of Fito that she said that if she would have had a son, she would have liked her son to be like Fito: courageous, handsome, intelligent, and successful. I, like many others, was suspicious as to the motivation of Fito and expressed our cautious position, stating that time would tell."

Ramon indicated that Fito was a deeply frustrated professional. He had no father figure to follow. He had deep resentment against the landlord who fathered him; he had no contacts with law firms, so therefore he could not open an office and practice law after he graduated from the university. He accepted a menial job at a second class newspaper where he received a small salary as a reporter. His wife divorced him and married a member of General Matista's cabinet. This was an insult to him. It is interesting to note that Fito never remarried. His first show of force was a military parade in front of his former wife's home on one of the beaches close to the Isla Grande capital.

Johnny asked Ramon, "Could you tell us what his relationship was with his sister?"

Ramon replied, "This is one of the tragic episodes of the revolution. Alex's wife became openly opposed to her brother's true intentions. Fito had warned her and because of her open criticism to the revolution, he ordered her execution (which happened by poisoning and drowning) and her body was found one morning floating in a small lake close to the beach section of the capital. This episode was labeled as a drowning accident. Alex knew well that it had been a deliberate assassination ordered by Lucia's brother.

Alex had several choices. One was to continue his successful practice. The other one was to become actively involved with the underground that became disenchanted with Fito. The third was to get away from the island. He decided to leave the island. He got all his papers related to his scientific research and succeeded in leaving the island with the pretext of attending a medical meeting that was to be held in the United States. Alex finally got out of Isla Grande and settled in Miami. He successfully passed the Florida Boards and Medical Boards following internship and a residency at the University Hospital in Miami. He practiced successfully as an internist. Alex invested in real estate and in a few years became quite wealthy."

Annie was starting to yawn but could not keep her eyes from her grandfather's face. They paused for a light lunch. They went on the deck and looked around again. The small boat was still floating, gently moving with the waves towards the shore of North Key Largo. Once again, there were apparently no survivors on site.

The three moved back into the lounge and Ramon continued his narration. "As you will see later, Annie, Alex became the brains behind a plot designed to topple Fito's government.

Years later he made it possible for your grandmother and me to come to the United States. You all may ask me why I am interested in this small vessel. There is a very interesting story behind it. The floating vessel motivated the story which followed this encounter.

I must tell you, Annie, that your grandmother and I came to Miami as a result of Alex's making a claim for us. We were lucky to join your mother, Lidia, and later, your father, Mario.

One of my dreams was to some day go fishing again. In Isla Grande, we were not allowed to have a boat. There was no such boat like a Bertram in all the island. Only Fito and some of the generals had large motorboats. Today is a very special day in my life. I wonder who the people were who used this small boat which reminds me of another Cucaracha? What happened to them? I pray to God that they made it safely to the United States. Let's go back in time."

CHAPTER 2

ISLA GRANDE: MUSIC AND DANCING

Ramon continued his narration, "A few years before Fito's revolution, my wife and I moved to the outskirts of Isla Grande's capital, Valencia. There were two families who were neighbors. We were interested in Lidia's education and wanted to be close to the capital. At this time, Lidia was 20 years of age and as I mentioned before, a beautiful brunette with long, wavy hair and sparkling black eyes, about 5'5" tall and blessed with a beautiful body. Our neighbors' son, Mario Gonzalez, was tall, slender, muscular, and had dark, straight hair. He also had bright, dark brown, expressive eyes.

At this time, Lidia was a school teacher at an elementary school, and Mario worked in a textile factory. Mario was 28 years old. They grew up together and had been friends since they were youngsters. Mario's parents were farmers who raised chickens, and had several cows and some pigs. Periodically, they sold eggs, milk, and meat to trusted friends and customers who came from the city and offered them "pesos." The scarcity of food products in the cities was such that many people came to the villages and visited farmers who had access to milk, eggs, meat, vegetables and fruits. The government, being the only legitimate buyer of food products, forbade the sale of these goods. They kept detailed records of the farm animals on the various farms as well as the crops. It was difficult and dangerous for the farmers to sell privately to those who eagerly paid large sums of money; a small pig could bring as many as 2000 pesos.

The only entertainment available to the villagers was folkloric music, listening to the radio, or celebrating some festivity in the nearby towns.

One evening, at one of these festivities, Lidia was approached by the head of a militia group, a vicious, husky man named Ivan, who later became one of Fito's closest "friends." He knew that Lydia was engaged to Mario, but nevertheless, made many attempts to convince her that he was the better choice. Lidia became upset at Ivan's advances. Mario was unaware of Ivan's intentions, though he knew that Lidia was a very popular person because of her beauty and charm. Many militia groups showed up at parties to spy and also to take advantage of the power they exerted upon civilians.

Ramon continued, "During this period of time, we all felt that because there was a single buyer, the government who controlled all our businesses, there was no incentive and no hopes in the foreseeable future to regain a democratic government.

The frustrations of people who were not sympathetic with the government prevailed throughout the island. Each community had a representative who acted as a watchman and reported any activity that might be construed as an opposition to the government. People were imprisoned without cause and their trials were markedly delayed.

We were helpless. We either had to actively become engaged in counter-revolutionary activities or live as passive bystanders, accepting and patiently waiting for positive changes to occur.

It is interesting how countries all over the world become informed of what is happening internally in many countries where there is a dictatorship. There is no mechanism to enforce legitimacy of the governments and to correct situations that lead to imprisonment and elimination of counter-revolutionaries.

At these gatherings, usually on a Saturday night, people would gather at a park located in almost the central part of the village. There was a musical band, consisting of a guitar and bongo players, very good singers, and couples who danced until late evening hours. This was an opportunity for singles to meet. Women would walk, following the same direction, opposite the young men. When they established eye contact, a conversation usually started, and they ended up dancing. This was the place where Lidia met Mario for the first time and both fell in love immediately. Lidia was an excellent dancer and Mario just followed her.

CHAPTER 3

LIDIA AND MARIO'S ROMANCE
AND THE PLANNING OF THEIR ESCAPE

"We lived close to the seaside. All the northern coast of Isla Grande is dotted with magnificent beaches; the most popular one is Valero Beach. Its airport receives direct flights from the United States, Canada, Latin American countries, Europe, and even Africa. Different from the Florida coast that did not have good beaches, the island of Isla Grande was blessed with marvelous beaches. Many foreign investors built luxury hotels in some of the keys close to the island as well as some of the beaches.

One evening, while holding hands, Mario and Lidia walked towards the nearby beach. When looking at the ocean, it appeared like a lake. There was no wind and very small waves that caressed the white sandy beach. The full moon was illuminating a trail in the water, which symbolically could be construed as the road to freedom. The clear skies were twinkling with millions of stars. It was a perfect evening.

He told her, "Today I was asked to relocate to another province for the harvesting of sugar cane. They haven't told me how long I'll be forced to work in the fields. I recently had a fight with the foreman of my factory. We argued about the unbearable restrictions placed upon the population of Isla Grande by the government. I suspect he was the person who gave my name to the local militia with the intention of punishing me. I'm fed up with this regime! I have decided that it is best to leave Isla Grande. Many of my best friends have already done so and successfully crossed the Florida Straits. I know the outcome is uncertain, but I have decided to leave."

While holding hands and whispering to each other, Lidia, who was caught by surprise, looked into Mario's eyes and said, "Oh, Mario, I am not surprised to hear what you are saying. We both have suffered rigors and disappointments. There is nothing we can do to promote changes in our way of life. More than anything else, I want you to know that I love you so much! I will follow wherever you go. Please tell me more. How and when do you plan to leave?" Lidia was visibly nervous. In the back of her mind were not only the possibilities of a dangerous trip, but also the repercussions of what the government would do to their families when they know that they have left the island. It was well known that because of those who leave the island, their parents and friends are often punished for allowing the "gusanos" (rebel Islanders) to leave the island.

Mario answered, "I will now give you some details of what I was planning. I have found a very small boat that unfortunately can only carry two people. It is so small, it can be lifted without help and carried to the beach by just one person. It will be enough. I plan to have drinking water and some basic food items. My plans are to leave at night, and because of the flow of the Gulfstream and the heavy traffic of ships, I will be spotted and taken to the Florida Keys. The weather must be good for this trip."

The prevailing winds of the islands of the Caribbean are southeast winds. The direction of the Gulfstream, which goes from south to north, paralleling the East Coast of the United States and the prevailing southeast winds allow for vessels to sail towards the United States along the eastern border. The only precaution is to watch for hurricane season which starts on June 1 and ends November 15, and also the winter months which provoke tall waves due to the opposing direction of the northern winds which oppose the northerly direction of the Gulfstream. Large waves build up and make the trip very treacherous. A combination of hurricane season and the disadvantage of the winter months suggest that the best time for making the trip are the months of April, May, and June.

Lidia said, "I will not let you leave me behind." Visibly worried and upset, she continued, "I never told you before, but I have been harassed by militiamen and if they realize that you're not around, they will make my life impossible. I do not mind the risk of the trip as long as I am with you! I love you and I will follow you wherever you go and whenever you want to leave. I beg you to take me." Big tears rolled down her cheeks and she hugged and kissed him.

After awhile, both walked into the small house where Mario's mother and Lidia's parents were chatting around a table, lit by a candle. These two families lived in comfortable, spacious, simple homes. They did not have the architecture of the house where Ramon used to live which had the typical Spanish style construction. These homes were relatively small but comfortable. Slanted roofs and colorful gardens gave them a picturesque appearance. They constituted an island of peace located not too far from where life was a constant turmoil.

Mario and Lidia's parents were drinking coffee and listening to a radio program which was being broadcast from the United States. The program was usually heard at night, although it transmitted 24 hours a day. The Isla Grande government forbade listening to radio stations transmitting from the United States.

Lidia and Mario walked into the room with joyful expressions. "What is happening, Lidia?" her father asked. "As you know, we have been engaged for quite some time," she replied. "We have decided to get married, but not here." Her eyes were sparkling and motivated anxious looks from their parents.

"What do you mean?" her father asked.

Lidia responded, "Mario wants us to marry . . . . in the United States; I have agreed!"

"Are you both crazy, or have you been drinking?" Lidia's father asked.

"No, sir." Mario replied. "I have decided to leave the island and have given Lidia the reasons; I have no choice. I am going to join the thousands who flee Isla Grande regularly and shall do so very soon."

"Mario, you never told me of your plans. What will I do after you leave me?" his mother asked.

"I know you are getting old, but, fortunately, you are healthy. I cannot risk your safety on the long, dangerous journey I will make. You will be taken care of by our relatives and Lidia's parents. We all belong to the same family. After we are settled, I will try to bring you all to the United States, as soon as humanly possible," Mario answered.

Lidia's mother, visibly upset, said, "Lydia, I hope that you are not planning to do something foolish."

"Mother, I have decided to go with Mario, no matter what happens," Lidia replied. "Please understand that the probabilities are high that we'll make it. We will carry adequate supplies of water and enough food for at least three to five days."

"This is outrageous!" Lidia's father interjected. "Why don't you wait for Mario to go alone and claim you later, the same way he is planning to do with his mother?"

"Father, I cannot stay here without Mario. My life will be in danger. I've been harassed by militiamen who have only been cautious because they know Mario is my fiancé. When they learn he has left the island they will label him a "gusano" and hurt me." Knowing their angry parents would try to discourage them, they turned around and quickly left the house.

Mario's and Lidia's parents remained, discussing among themselves the pros and cons of what they had just heard. They did not reach an agreement. Some felt it was too dangerous and not a trip for a young woman. Others felt that their choice of remaining was a poor one as well.

Mario took Lidia into a low-lying area of shrubbery. There he showed her an old, small, wooden boat about five feet long and two and one-half feet wide. It was camouflaged under the foliage of several trees. "The name of the boat is "Cucaracha," Mario said.

"Why Cucaracha?" Lidia inquired.

"Because it resembles a bug," Mario responded, "and it reminds me of the old Isla Grande song of the bug that couldn't walk because it lacked legs. The legs of this bug will be the oars which I will use to take the bug to the United States."

"When do you expect to leave?" Lidia asked.

"I would like to take advantage of the 28th of July festivities, when most of the Isla Grande government leaders and the Armed Forces will be distracted, and leave on the night of July the 27th," Mario answered. They kissed again and walked slowly towards the beach. It was a beautiful evening. The moon could be seen on the horizon. Calm waters again made the ocean appear like a lake. They both thought that they would be lucky if the conditions of the seas were the same as the ones they were looking at.

CHAPTER 4

MEETING AT THE HEADQUARTERS
OF THE ISLA GRANDE GOVERNMENT

On a bright sunny morning in the early spring of 1999, a motorcade was seen approaching the Headquarters of the Isla Grande government in the capital. It was an old building that had been in existence for about fifty years. It faced the Bay and at a distance, one could see erected statues and a beautiful lawn where people gathered at night, escaping from the heat in homes where they had no air-conditioning. Three Mercedes and a dozen motorcycles escorted Ricardo, the Major General of the Isla Grande Armed Forces. The streets leading to Valencia's Presidential Palace were deserted.

Ricardo was 5'6" tall. He had receding hair and was always dressed in a military uniform. He was Fito's youngest brother, who never expressed interest in a university career. He joined the Armed Forces after the Revolution and Fito made him the

Commander-in-Chief, based not on his knowledge, but on his loyalty to Fito.

Soldiers were posted on the roofs of the buildings surrounding the Palace, as well as in concealed locations on the streets. Ricardo walked into the Palace, accompanied by four assistants, all dressed in military uniforms. After passing through the main gate, they yielded their weapons which were then placed in a storage area. They walked through the metal detector and towards an elevator that led to the fourth floor. Only uniformed personnel were observed in the inside of the building.

Armed, uniformed, young soldiers of Fito's private army lined the corridors and operated the elevator. Fito was notorious for replacing his personal guard, always using young soldiers who had very little training but were loyal to him and were handsomely compensated. Most of Fito's closest allies during the Revolution had been killed or had disappeared mysteriously. He felt protected by using young men, usually farmers, with ambitions and well remunerated by Fito himself. Ricardo entered the elevator with his assistants and proceeded to the fourth floor which was the main government reception and office area. They walked to the door that opened into the meeting room where his brother, Fito, was waiting. At the door, two of Fito's guards used a hand-held metal detecting wand and performed a second search of Ricardo and his assistants. After confirming that they carried no metallic weapons, they were led into the room. These were standing orders that applied even to the Head of the Armed Forces. The room was wood-paneled. There were books on the shelves and one large painting of the first President of Isla Grande was displayed behind the desk that sat in the center of the room. There was a sofa in front of the desk and comfortable leather-lined brown chairs which matched the brown desk.

Fito was sitting behind a large, hand-carved desk crowded with dozens of papers and envelopes. He appeared tired and, as always, poorly groomed. He was dressed in his usual green military uniform, with his trademark open collar. His eyes were bleary. Circles around his eyes attested to partying and a short night's sleep.

He did not stand or acknowledge his visitors, except for a cursory nod to Ivan, a favorite, who was always present when Fito received visitors. Ricardo remained standing, as did his assistants. Visibly nervous, he greeted his brother, who had one guard standing at each side. "Early this morning, a tugboat departed from Reina and was intercepted by our Coast Guard just beyond the Light House," Ricardo said. "On board, there were over 60 people including 23 children and some old "gusanos". Our patrol boats used hoses and water at high pressure to punish the escapees. One of the boats struck the stern of the tugboat, sinking it. We rescued some of the "gusanos", but many, including children, (he paused) drowned.

I fear this episode will become an international scandal. In the first six months of this year, over 5,000 "gusanos" have reached the coasts of Florida. This number probably represents less than 30% of those who attempted the journey. The majority have lost their lives.

"On Isla Grande's radio stations in Miami, in a Hispanic newspaper, and on U.S. TV stations, interviews with some of the "gusanos" who escaped have been extensively publicized. Last week, a 14-year-old child was rescued by the U.S. Coast Guard. He was taken to the City Hospital in Miami where he related to the American Press how he saw his parents drown. They drowned because the only life jacket available was given to him. Tugboats, ferry boats, and even an Isla Grande Coast Guard vessel joined the parade of small vessels (rafts, improvised vessels made from roofs of buses, boards, including wooden doors, and surfboards, assembled on rubber tires with primitive sails, etc.). This latest incident will be used by our enemies to further discredit the revolution.

I need not remind you of the defection of some of our pilots and the diversion of commercial and tourist aircrafts to the United States.

Fito, visibly upset, addressed Ricardo, "We have a bunch of incompetent Coast Guards who, rather than patrolling our coast, are most of the time drunk and partying. I know that we have very few vessels and they work very inefficiently."

Ricardo said, "Our Isla Grande Coast Guard is limited, we have very few available vessels to patrol our coast and there is a severe shortage of fuel. We cannot maintain a 24-hour surveillance. Needless to say, our desperate economic situation which affects so many Islanders is the major motive forcing thousands of people to leave the island."

Ricardo knew that the best way of dealing with Fito was to listen and not argue.

Fito listened to Ricardo's presentation, first with a passive attitude, then at the end of Ricardo's speech, he reacted violently, shouting and cursing.

"You are a bunch of incompetent SOB's who don't know how to carry out your jobs. I profoundly hate these Islanders who do not help our revolution and react impatiently and stupidly, encouraged by those bastards in exile who just want to return to Isla Grande to exploit us and enrich themselves."

He stormed out of the room, leaving behind his astonished associates. He had offered no solution to Ricardo's comments.

Fito was not always at the Palace and met infrequently with Ricardo. He knew of Ricardo's loyalty, but felt that all aspects of security should be dealt by personnel he had hired to protect him and the integrity of the government. He did not pay too much attention to the statements made by Ricardo, so the magnitude of the deficiencies was downplayed by Fito.

CHAPTER 5

A SPECIAL PARTY FOR THE ELITE
OF THE ISLA GRANDE GOVERNMENT

Periodically, Fito entertained ambassadors from other countries and representatives of major investment companies. He was anxious to show a different image of Isla Grande by having selected guests stay at mansions that have been taken away from previous owners who have fled the country and been converted into deluxe office space or exquisite homes. Fito was also acutely aware of the need of importing dollars. One way was to foster tourism and the other was to allow investments whereby the foreign investor will own 49% of the property and 51% will be owned by Isla Grande's government.

That same evening, at the International Hotel, a party was being sponsored by Fito's Government. The International Hotel was a charming old hotel built on a hill and surrounded by beautiful gardens. There was a spectacular view of the bay from several terraces and from ocean view rooms. Tall, stately royal palms lined each side of the drive on the approach to the hotel.

Some old cars that dated back to the 1950's lined the driveways to the hotel. Some were hardtops and some convertibles. This display of automobiles was to show tourists the opportunity that they had to tour the island in these antiques that were very well kept and chauffeured by reliable government employees. The party was scheduled to start at 7:00 p.m.

Fito and his motorcade arrived at 9:00 p.m. He and Ricardo were escorted by several Mercedes limousines and Jeeps with mounted machine guns, accompanied by several dozen motorcycle policemen. Fito was dressed in the same green, wrinkled uniform he had been wearing all day. For this occasion, however, he wore a black tie and a white shirt. His face displayed a poorly groomed beard. He appeared vigorous; his eyes were sparkling and alert; an indication that he had taken a long nap that afternoon.

In the main ballroom, a large number of Isla Grande government representatives, all dressed in military uniforms, exchanged conversation with elegantly attired diplomats and foreign businessmen. The wrinkled, poorly fitted uniforms of the military personnel contrasted sharply with that of the diplomats and their companions. One particular person who caught Fito's attention was Hassan Nader, the Alcanian Ambassador to Isla Grande. He was a man about 50 years of age, about 5'11" inches tall. He had a very well-trimmed beard and was somewhat heavy, with tanned skin. He was dressed impeccably in a black silk suit and wore a green ceremonial sash that crossed from his right shoulder to his left hip. From the pocket of his jacket, numerous small medals and insignias were displayed, indicating the honors he had received from his country and others.

What attracted Fito's attention was not just the Ambassador, but Eva, his lovely, beautiful companion. She was elegantly tall and had straight long blond hair and a beautiful, but rather cold-looking face. Eva's tight, heavily sequined evening gown adapted snugly to her attractive, provocative figure, producing a symphony of fluid movement. Eva Kabor was also born and raised in Alcania. She studied languages and was able to speak Spanish fluently.

An orchestra played soft Latin music. Dictator Fito greeted all the important attendees to the Ball. They were all dressed in tuxedos or wearing uniforms. The Ball was being held on the main terrace of the hotel, overlooking the bay. As the hotel was on a hill, one could see the ocean all the way to the entrance to the Bay where a flashing light was on permanent display. Fito greeted some old friends he had met in Spain during his last visit. They were investing in the tourist industry. One was opening a chain of Spanish restaurants. Another represented the Spanish chain of hotels, which had built several hotels in Isla Grande, having over 2,700 rooms. An agreement had just been signed to build another resort in the famous Valero Beach area at a cost of approximately seventeen million dollars. Fifty percent would be financed by the Isla Grande government.

Fito appeared pleased and in the mood to enjoy another evening of excellent food, liquor, and entertainment. He met a delegation from Canada who were bringing large groups of tourists to the area of Valero Beach, and other new tourist resorts throughout the island. Tourism represented one of Isla Grande's largest booming industries. Some Central and South American businessmen and a group of Africans were also present. The latter wore the most conspicuous, attractive attire.

The dictator riveted his eyes on Eva, who coolly greeted him. Fito asked for the pleasure of dancing with her, but she refused, saying she had difficulty dancing to Latin music. Throughout the evening, the dictator couldn't take his eyes from the blonde Alcanian. Hors d'oeuvres and many rounds of whiskey, wine and rum-containing drinks were served until about 11:00 p.m., followed by a succulent elegantly served banquet. The party lasted until 2:00 in the morning. This food, available only to the elite of the Isla Grande government and foreigners, was in sharp contrast to the scarcity of food products available to the average Islander. Hassan and Eva spent a great deal of time talking to Ricardo, Fito's brother. They sat at the same table. The acquaintance would later prove to be very useful to Hassan.

Most of the attendees stayed at the hotel and others were staying at hotels that several decades before had casinos and luxurious lobbies and guest rooms.

The party ended around 3:00 a.m.

CHAPTER 6

ORDEALS OF ISLA GRANDE FAMILIES;
THE ISLA GRANDE CRISIS

Rationing had existed in Isla Grande for 50 years. Some families raised chickens on the roofs of their homes or in their backyards. The black market was an essential industry where goods were sold, others bought with U.S. dollars obtained from tourist tips and from relatives abroad. Theft was a serious problem and was motivated by the scarcity of goods, and the hunger of the Islanders. Most buildings and houses were poorly kept because of lack of paint, nails, and construction equipment, and the apathy of the dwellers.

The water supply was deficient and fresh water was often polluted with sewage. Rivers, lakes and the ocean were polluted from the dumping of raw sewage. The chronic lack of fuel prevented the maintenance of necessary pressure in the water supply system. Many Islanders suffered from a variety of illnesses, particularly diarrhea. Accumulations of water created a nidus for mosquitoes and a proliferation of tropical insects.

Throughout the island there was no pest control and insects, flies, and rats contaminated the cities and villages. The limited transport system of buses, trucks, and trains was unbearably crowded. The majority of Islanders transported themselves by walking and using bicycles. Hospitals were poorly supplied with medication, food, and covers for the sick. Relatives of patients were requested to bring linens, pillows, as well as food, and occasionally, even medication, to hospitals. Medical care was free; however surgical sutures, medical equipment, and medication were very scarce.

Islanders were rightfully upset when they compared two of their largest hospitals which were well-equipped and well-staffed, to the dire conditions of the hospitals and clinics used by the majority of Islanders throughout the island. Those hospitals were for the exclusive use of tourists and the elite of the Isla Grande government and a very important tourist medical industry had been established in Isla Grande. Isla Grande's government advertised in many Latin American cities the availability of medical and surgical treatments at very low cost. Vaccines and other products had been exported and marketed as examples of the high technological developments in Isla Grande, particularly biotechnology. In the early 90's, a large supply of vaccines was returned by Brazil with the complaint of their ineffectiveness.

The black market was rampant. Trading of goods, smuggling of products from small villages into large cities, theft, and fights were widespread. A special police force, called Rapid Reacting Brigades, wore civilian garb and responded promptly to situations where groups of Islanders either protested, fought, or gathered suspiciously in homes or on the streets.

Blackouts occurred periodically, and extended for weeks or months. At the time of blackouts, Islanders often vandalized stores. In many cities, walls had graffiti such as "Down with the Revolution," "We Need Liberty," "Fito, It's Enough," etc. As time went by, living conditions steadily deteriorated.

The population of Isla Grande in 1960 was six million people. About two million had since left the island. In 1982, over 125,000 Islander refugees were brought to the United States. In the early part of 1994, thousands also fled the country in man-made, primitive rafts.

In 1990, The Rescue Brothers started flying search and rescue patrols over the Florida Straits. Through August of 1998, they carried out over 2,500 missions, assisting the U.S. Coast Guard in the rescue of close to 37,000 people. Just in the month of August 1994, over 17,000 rafters were rescued in the Florida Straits.

A reporter wrote for one of the Miami newspapers in a column called "Balsa Vacia"—the empty raft: "The massive exodus of Islanders in anything that would float is the greatest act of rejection that a country can inflict on its government which has deprived them of their human rights, and the basic ingredients of a life with dignity."

The reporter further stated, "Not only has the social unit of the Islanders been destroyed, but also the central nucleus that constitutes the Isla Grande family." One rafter made the comment that he preferred "an end with horror rather than horror without an end."

Members of families had been dispersed. Many who settled abroad often did not know the whereabouts of their relatives. Some had drowned or were attacked by sharks. Others were in detention camps, the civilized version of a concentration camp. This massive exodus in protest of the dictatorship of Fito contrasted with the era before communism. The Islanders were never prone to migrate. On the contrary, they welcomed those who wished to live and settle in Isla Grande. Foreigners were received as new members of the extended Isla Grande family.

It was ironic that those who succeeded in leaving the island were picked up by the U.S. Coast Guard and returned to Isla Grande, to an American Naval Base.

The fear of the US Government was that a mass migration would occur. A high-ranking officer of the State Department who specializes in Isla Grande's affairs stated: "The arrival of tens, if not hundreds, of thousands of Isla Grande's citizens over a short period of time is a scenario that any US administration would like to avoid at all cost.

Some recently arrived immigrants said that they left because of uncertainty as to the future of the Island following the disappearance of the dictator.

According to a university study between October 2005 and September 2007 almost 77,000 Isla Grande citizens reached US soil, more than twice the number during the 1994 rafter exodus.

This same study notes that in the last seven years more Isla Grande's citizens have arrived than during the combined 1980 boat lift and the 1994 rafter exodus: 191,000 since 2000 vs. 162,191.

Countries run by a dictator sooner or later rebel. When human rights don't exist, the chronicity of the process leads to the exodus of citizens. The United States has been a haven for exiles. Thousands risk their lives, particularly crossing the Gulfstream. It has been stated that one out of eight make it to the mainland. Those that are captured by Coast Guards are returned to their home country where they are punished and most often disappear. As long as there are dictators there will be opposition and every attempt should be made to restore peace, democracy, and dignity.

CHAPTER 7

CONSTRUCTION OF BLACKSHARK

Alex Martin was a successful physician in exile who owned a 40' open fishing boat. He acquired his boat from the Mag Company. On a sunny day in Miami, Alex took his book to the Mag Company for a maintenance check-up. While at the factory he learned of a special boat called Blackshark which was a specially designed 40' boat. He arrived at the dock in North Miami, on a street known as Thunderboat Row, where the finest high-performance boat companies in the world reside.

After tying up his boat at the dock, Alex casually walked into the factory, as he had done on many previous occasions, particularly when his own boat was under construction. Alex had purchased his boat with the idea of cruising the Florida and Bahama islands and someday going back to Isla Grande and go fishing along the North Coast. His boat had the capability of being a fishing boat as well as a cruiser. Alex was much more than just a client to the employees of the Mag Company. He was a great friend to everyone there and was greatly admired, especially by Simon Thomas, the factory's chief engineer and the many Hispanic employees who considered him a role model. Alex knew virtually every employee on a first name basis and considered each one a friend. That was his nature.

This visit was much different from his previous visits. As Alex walked into the factory, he eyed a large black boat hull, much like that of his own 40 feet long boat, with a deep V and a racing hull. But there was something distinctly unique about this boat other than its color. A massive aluminum structure was being lowered by a crane into the cabin area. This was an area normally reserved for plush sofas and wet bars.

Simon halted the crane and walked over to welcome Alex. Simon was a well-built, 5'11" strong man with dark, wavy hair, fair skin, and a pleasant disposition. Typically, their conversations began with greetings and a short conversation, followed by preparation of a service order. But this time Alex was consumed with curiosity about the boat under construction. Alex could see that Simon was bursting with pride.

"This is the most exciting project any boat builder could ever undertake," Simon exclaimed, "and the fact that we were chosen to participate is the greatest compliment any boat builder could ever hope for."

Simon went on to explain that the marketing strategists at Mag Company, the world's largest defense contractor, had decided that the time was right to enter another arena in the defense industry. With the demise of the Soviet Union, the days of big battleships were over. Maritime conflicts of the future would be regional, such as the Persian Gulf War, i.e. "reach out and touch me wars."

Years ago, Ivan Suarez, who is now Fito's right-hand man, had proven this very same concept. They sent out small, fast boats to fire rocket propelled grenades at the big American battleships which were escorting oil tankers through the Persian Gulf. Their little boats were almost impossible to detect on radar and were extremely effective in demonstrating their destructive capabilities. Battleships were just big lumbering dinosaurs that made easy targets.

Mag Company had decided to apply their expertise in aviation weapons systems to relatively small, high-performance boats. Mag was chosen to participate in the project because of its reputation for building strong, fast hulls, with good handling characteristics in rough seas. Mag's fiberglass hulls would be difficult to detect on radar and they were, by far, the most experienced company using reliable, high-performance diesel power.

Mag's expertise was not only that of an equipment supplier, but also as specialists in systems integrators. In designing any given "system," they would evaluate each component not only on its own capabilities, but also on its compatibility with the other system components. The objective was synergy. This was a great improvement over the manner in which governments would typically equip a patrol boat with a hodge-podge approach. The most critical components of the Mag Company patrol boat system were aviation systems that had a proven track record on the Apache helicopter. Such a system was utilized during the Gulf War allowing pilots to lock their cross hairs on building air ducts and score perfect hits.

Blackshark was to be equipped with virtually the same machinery. "The trick," as Simon explained it, "was to adapt aviation equipment in such a manner that it could survive the high level impact of a hull crashing into heavy seas at high speed and survive the corrosive salt water environment."

Alex was fascinated by the concept and impressed with the aggressiveness of Mag Company to venture into this type of project. In the back of his mind, he could not help but think of how the destructive capabilities of such a machine could actually be used to serve mankind. After all, this was a machine built by the "good guys," to be used by the "good guys" to defeat terrorists and protect freedom-loving people.

"I understand the concept," Alex said to Simon, "but how does it actually work?"

Simon was thrilled to see Alex's interest and was pleased to continue describing the vessel. He said, "Blackshark has radar which picks up a target. The eyeball, which is a white ball mounted on the radar arch, directs an infrared beam towards the target. This allows for a visual demonstration of the target. This gives the operator an opportunity to identify the target. The picture can be zoomed in for better identification."

"Even though Blackshark is jumping over the waves, the picture is as steady as your television monitor. A laser, also mounted in the eyeball, locks on the target. It feeds information back to a bank of computers that calculate the relative speed and heading of the target."

Alex commented, "This is amazing. I never understood how you can overcome the impact of waves that result in the jumping of the vessel and be able to destroy a target."

Simon continued, "The computer bank calculates the lead distance and trajectory of the rounds to be fired from the onboard cannon and even figures in windage, temperature and humidity, which all affect the accuracy of the rounds. The computer then directs the M230 30 mm remotely turreted cannon onto the target and holds it precisely in position to fire at any time. The cannon is also stabilized so that it is not affected by the up and down movements of the boat while it is underway. In fact, the cannon actually moves so fast that your eye cannot follow it, movement which counters the action of the boat in the sea."

"The gunner simply stands at a console in the boat, watches the video, and can fire with pinpoint accuracy simply aiming the cannon with a switch and pushing a red button labeled "fire." The cannon can spit out 650 rounds per minute. The rounds are about one pound each and carry unbelievable destructive power."

"We saw videos of the same cannon mounted on tanks, blowing down concrete walls," exclaimed Simon with excitement. "This is the most awesome machine in its class in the world. In fact, it's a prototype. No Navy in the world has a small, fast, coastal patrol boat with this sort of capability."

Alex commented, "Simon, I am very excited, please tell me more."

"In addition to the cannon, the vessel has a gunwale-mounted, crew-served machine gun. The hull of the boat would have an open cockpit to provide an unobstructed field of view for the operators and allow quick access to the forward deck for rapid boarding of adversary craft. As with your boat, the main cabin area contains the electronic rack, galley, head/shower, and bunks. This compartment is air-conditioned for electronics cooling and personal comfort.

"The engine room contains the propulsion plant, electrical plant, and auxiliary systems. I know you store all your tools, a safety raft for six passengers, the EPIRB unit (for transmitting signals in the event the boat capsizes), and an electrical reel. Obviously, we are not going to go fishing with Blackshark!"

Alex asked Simon, "How many people are needed to operate Blackshark? Simon replied:

"To safely operate Blackshark in all conditions, there is a need for three people: a helmsman, navigator, and an engineer. Each crew member has an assigned control to monitor his or her respective areas of concern. All crew and passenger stations are equipped with bolster seats that provide protection and restraint for the occupant for the full range of craft motion and speeds, including sudden impact shock and vibration.

As you know, all our hulls have a deep V configuration (24 degrees at transom). This substantially reduces shock, adding to crew/passenger comfort. Like with your boat, Blackshark uses twin diesel engines and Arneson surface drives which have above a large diving platform. There is an arch in the cockpit to provide optimum sensor height and clearance for antenna, radar, and passive surveillance system mountings. You have in your boat a GPS, two antennae and spotlights. These same items are installed in Blackshark. This is a very strong arch because it must support the weight of the antenna, the sensor systems, cabling, and hoses."

"Blackshark has a radar-based system that detects and recognizes potential targets that are either identified visually or by means of the radar. I want to repeat this special feature of Blackshark. The Mag Company has developed a special electro-optical surveillance system. It is a lightweight, multi-sensor imaging system which consists of infrared sensor and an eye-safe laser range finder. The sensors are all installed on a highly stabilized turret which isolates the system from shock, vibration, and motion induced by the craft. There is a high-resolution television system that is used for target detection and recognition during dawn, day, and dusk. The special infrared sensor is used at night, providing infrared imagery of the scene. There is accurate range information for weapons control and to aid in safe navigation. The images are adequately displayed on protected screens from sunlight."

"The vessel has state-of-the-art components which allow the navigator to obtain information for safe navigation at high speeds. A central processor is used to gather information from the GPS receiver (a type of Loran which uses satellites to plot exact location in a very accurate way). Depth finder, speed, radar and GPS information are all gathered and manipulated by a central processor. Electronic charts are used, rather than wet charts. This allows the navigator to clearly identify moving targets while the craft is cruising at variable speeds."

"At all times, one can establish the heading, position, distance to travel, way points, speed information and depth. One can use the cannon and machine gun to precisely hit targets within an established range from the vessel."

Alex then made a comment, "Simon, what you have described is too much to digest. I get the general idea which explains why this is a unique vessel in the world."

Simon replied, "You are right, Alex. As you can see, this 40' boat adapted with the sophisticated weapons and electronic system, is the most unique vessel ever constructed. During day and night, coastal waters and oceans can be patrolled. The range of the vessel with its 400 gallon two diesel tanks is about 350 miles. The gas consumption is about 1.12 gallons per nautical mile. The hull is constructed in such a way that if it would hit, for example, a floating barrel, it will not make a hole, and the vessel would not sink. There are very few vessels on the market that have this reinforced hull. Without the weapons and electronic controls, the vessel weighs 35,000 pounds."

Alex and Simon continued discussing the vessel. He subsequently asked Simon, the Chief Engineer, if it was possible to reinforce the hull. He told Simon, "In the event that Blackshark encounters enemy vessels, the hull must be strong enough to tolerate the impact of bullets from machine guns fired from shore or from another vessel. Also, you must reinforce the deck of the boat. It is conceivable that from an aircraft, such as a helicopter, bullets can be fired in an attempt to blow up the vessel. These are the reasons the hull and the deck must be well protected."

Alex asked Simon if he could develop a special magnetic diversion system in the hull. Alex said to Simon, "Torpedoes can be fired to sink Blackshark. They may come from another vessel or from a submarine. By having a magnetic diversion system incorporated in the hull, incoming metallic objects could be diverted. In this way, the vessel will be safe from torpedoes. Obviously, there is a limit to how much the vessel can take and bazookas or cannons can destroy the vessel, indeed."

"Simon," said Alex, "Another device should be installed on the vessel. A smoke screen device will become very useful in the event Blackshark is chased by an aircraft. In the radar arch, you must install a device that will release smoke which will cover a large area in front, behind, above, and to the sides of the vessel with the purpose of disguising the vessel. If Blackshark is chased by an aircraft, the smoke screen will be activated. Remember, it will be tricky to create a smoke screen in front of the vessel, due to the air blowing in the opposite direction of the vessel. Smoke capsules will have to be fired in a fan-like arrangement in front and to the sides of the vessel, and when they reach a certain altitude, smoke will be released from the capsules. My thoughts are that when the smoke screen is activated, any aircraft flying over Blackshark will see underneath a large cloud. Visually, the aircraft will be unable to see the exact location of Blackshark."

Simon said, "I designed a specially designed helmet and bullet-proof garment to be included with the vessel." This had been a separate project and kept secretly from the Board of Directors of the Mag Company.

Alex was amazed and actually quite proud of himself that his close friend had become involved in such a project. In fact, Alex's mind was so focused on Blackshark that he left without giving instructions for the service work on his own boat and had to call back the following day.

CHAPTER 8

SIMON, THE CHIEF ENGINEER

Alex first met Simon Thomas, the Chief Engineer of the Mag Company, when he bought one of their boats earlier. He became acquainted with Simon and admired him. Simon was considered by all who knew him as a most talented and honest individual. Intrigued to explore his past, Alex invited Simon to a Latin meal. They met at one of the most popular restaurants in Miami. After the dinner, Alex asked, "Simon, what is your background?"

"I was raised in Isla Grande in a poor, hard-working family," Simon replied. "I went to the Polytechnic Institute in the capital where I earned a degree in engineering. I joined the Isla Grande Air Force in 1968 and was sent to Angola, Africa as a member of an Isla Grande battalion."

"As you know, Fito "volunteered" Isla Grande's troops and technicians to other countries. Islanders sent to work abroad were paid a fixed salary. The Isla Grande government received many thousands of dollars in exchange for manpower provided by the Islanders. As a member of the Armed Forces, we were paid the equivalent of three to four hundred dollars a month. Each of us represented at least $1,000 a month to the Isla Grande government. For years, physicians have been offered at a cost of about $2,000 a month. They are paid 10 to 20% of this amount and the government keeps the difference."

"As you know, our presence in Africa and in other countries was not for idealistic purposes, but as another business of the government. I participated in more than twenty military assaults and in the last one, my shoulder was injured. After two years in Angola, I returned to Isla Grande and continued in the Air Force."

"Shortly after arriving in Isla Grande, while visiting my family, I saw my father among a group of protestors. Members of the Rapid Action Brigade fought and dissolved this rebellious group which was protesting about the lack of food. My father was beaten terribly.

"When I got to the scene, the militia had already departed with the leaders of the group who were imprisoned. They left many injured, innocent Islanders unattended, who didn't deserve the physical punishment inflicted upon them. The leader of the Brigade was the infamous sergeant, Ivan. I don't know if this was his original name or one he adopted when he received a military degree in Russia."

"This episode motivated me more than ever to leave the country. I picked up my father, took him home, but shortly thereafter, he died. My mother had died the year before. I have only one younger brother, Tony, who was, at that time, a member of the local militia."

Tony had some resemblance to Simon. He was about 5'10 ½" tall, not as strong-looking as Simon, but with a very pleasant look and an easygoing personality.

"When I told him that I was leaving the country for the United States, he begged me to bring him with me. We made careful plans and assembled a small boat. One night, we took the wooden boat to the beach. It had a single outboard engine and a sail which I had built. We loaded it with gasoline, water, crackers, honey, bread, and smoked fish. We went into the water, dressed in dark clothes, and our faces stained black. We pushed the boat into the ocean. After swimming about two miles off the coast, while pushing the boat ahead of us, we boarded the boat and started rowing. When we felt we were far enough away, we turned on the engine and were lucky it carried us about 35 miles; the rest of the trip was without the motor."

"We set sail and the southeast winds took us to the coast of Marathon Key, which, as you know, is between Miami and Key West. Close to land, we were picked up by the U.S. Coast Guard. After going through the usual personal, medical checkups, and immigration procedures, we were released."

"We had an elderly aunt who had come to the United States in the early 60's. Her husband worked at one of the Miami factories and died a few years later. We started doing menial jobs and took English lessons at night."

"A friend of my aunt said that the expertise I developed with engines and electronics could be used by a boat-building company. We were both interviewed by the owner of the Mag Company, who told me that I could work at the factory on a trial basis. I asked them to hire Tony as my assistant, which they did. This was ten years ago."

"Since that time, my brother and I have been working there and I have the position of leader of an engineering team which has built all types of vessels. Recently, I designed a boat to be used for patrolling. You may have seen it in the factory, or at least at last year's International Boat Show. With our engineering staff and that of the Mag Corporation, we have installed in this vessel the most sophisticated equipment that anyone could ever imagine."

"Simon, I admire your risking your lives by leaving Isla Grande to reach the coast of the United States," Alex commented. "You're a living example of where talent and hard work can lead. If you have the talent, perseverance, and are given the opportunity to develop yourself, success can be achieved in the environment of the U.S. Everyone speaks very highly of you. What are your greatest wishes and goals in life?"

"Neither Tony nor I have married. He is still my baby brother," Simon replied. "I believe that I've reached an age when I should marry soon. One reason I haven't married and have no children is that I would like to get rid of the bastard who remains stubbornly in power in Isla Grande. I've been working in the underground in my spare time. I would like to see democracy re-established in Isla Grande as soon as humanly possible. I don't want to risk the well-being of a wife and my children. This is why I haven't married."

"What would you say if you were put in a position where you could succeed in your goals, giving to millions the opportunity of living in a free country, making a million dollars, and doing all this at a minimum risk to you," Alex asked. "Would you be interested?"

"Absolutely", Simon answered.

"Well, then, listen carefully," Alex said. "The project we have is as follows. One of your patrol boats must be specially built for this project. The construction of what we will name Blackshark must be completed by this coming July 1st. Do you think you can do this?"

"You can bet on it!" Simon answered.

"After the vessel is built, you and two of your associates must test the vessel and teach three people, whom I'll tell you about later, in the use of the weapons and all the operation features of Blackshark," Alex continued. "On July 28th you will undertake the second phase of the Blackshark project and must be in full control of the vessel to carry out its mission. I'll tell you more later about Phase 2, and upon completion, you'll be paid one million dollars."

"I agree to these two phases and would like my brother to join me in this project," Simon replied.

"Simon, I request that you discuss this project with no one, including your younger brother, until Phase 2 is close to being implemented. For the time being, I prefer to withhold the most important part of the mission."

They shook hands, and the meeting ended.

Alex was just waiting for a meeting with close friends who would collectively finance the project and a person who was able to contact the Chief and Commander of Isla Grande's Armed Forces. These two elements were essential for the success of the Omega Project.

CHAPTER 9

THE AMBASSADOR OF ALCANIA

Every year in South Florida, there are International Boat Shows. One is held in Fort Lauderdale, a city north of Miami and the other one is in Miami Beach. All types of boats are displayed and there are visitors coming from all parts of the world.

The previous year, at an International Boat Show in Miami Beach, Hassan Nader, the Ambassador of Alcania to Isla Grande, was introduced to Alex by a common friend, Hakkim, a Saudi Arabian client of the Mag Company. Hassan came to Miami using a Saudi Arabian passport. Hakkim, Hassan and Alex had lunch together and Alex came to realize how smart and ambitious Hassan was. The next day, Alex took Hassan to a private club located on North Biscayne Boulevard, not too far from where the International Boat Show was being Held, to chat privately.

"Hakkim, our mutual friend, has told me that you are a very clever, successful businessman," Alex said. "How do you like living in Isla Grande?"

"To be frank with you," Hassan answered, "I live in a beautiful home which was confiscated by the government and with excellent company. I live lavishly and admire and enjoy your wonderful weather and your beautiful beaches. However, we are surrounded by poverty and filth. It sickens me to see the living conditions of most Islanders. It is difficult to imagine that there is so much suffering and poverty so close to the United States. Our maid regularly takes leftover food to her family, which, like so many others, is starving."

"I see young, lovely Islander women prostituting their bodies for a few dollars or for food. Isla Grande requests visitors from other countries to buy goods in stores only open for tourists and visitors. The suffering that surrounds us is depressing. The streets and buildings are run-down. No one wants to improve or repair their surroundings. I wish for a better life for all, but, at this time, I don't see how a change can be made."

"Hassan, you didn't enjoy the Isla Grande of the 50's and the 60's," Alex said. "Isla Grande was always called the Jewel of America. Our peso was at par with the U.S. dollar. Contrary to all the government sponsored propaganda you may have heard, Isla Grande had a large, strong, enthusiastic, hard-working middle-class. The population in the 60's was a little over six million people. The Islanders who came from Africa represented about 12%. There were private clubs, but I can assure you that we never discriminated against neither the blacks nor the Chinese, nor any other individuals. Jokingly, we used to call most Europeans who lived in Isla Grande, "Pollacks." Few were from Poland. However, we used to kid with this group of industrious, hard-working Europeans, and made jokes about them, using the nickname Pollacks."

"The United States did not exploit the Islanders. As with other industrialized countries, they established business relationships wherever conditions were favorable. They took advantage of socio-economical situations, but they did nothing illegal or unacceptable. Islanders often preferred to work for American companies as they paid the highest salaries. No business deals were made among countries unless they were sanctioned by the government of that specific country."

"Beautiful hotels were built in the 50's and 60's. Many of the casinos in these hotels competed with the luxury and entertainment of those in Las Vegas and the Bahamas. We never experienced an increase in the crime rate because of the casinos. There was a lottery allowed for the population at large, as you see here in the United States. Isla Grande's professionals were among the most outstanding workers in this hemisphere."

"In the 60's, approximately close to 3,000 of the 6,000 Isla Grande physicians migrated to the United States; they were all welcomed. Many joined academic institutions and have had outstanding careers. Numerous Isla Grande-Americans became professors at distinguished universities throughout the nation. Engineers, lawyers, economists, and many other professionals have done exceedingly well in the United States. Some relocated to countries in Central and South America and Europe."

"The population in 1998 was estimated to be 6,620,000. Sixty percent were born since the revolution. The capital of Isla Grande had a population of 1,290,000."

"Hassan, the exodus of Islanders has exceeded two million out of the six million population in 1960. Obviously, the majority who left the island didn't exclusively represent the wealthy and middle classes. In South Florida there are over one and a half million Isla Grande-Americans. They have formed a closely-knit society that has been fortunate to find in the United States, a generous country in which to settle, work and prosper."

"Historically, Isla Grande had offered opportunity to everyone. Our unemployment was negligible. Free public schools and medical care were available to any poor Isla Grande citizen. It is not true that universal health care and education are major accomplishments of Fito's regime. It is true, however, that schools are available in every region of the island."

"At Isla Grande University, academic positions were obtained through competitive contests. In the United States, people are appointed to become assistant, associate, or full professors. In Isla Grande, you were examined and your credentials carefully reviewed. Only through credentialing and tough examinations did professionals obtain academic positions."

"Spain ruled Isla Grande for four centuries. The United States occupied Isla Grande militarily for three years before Isla Grande became a Republic. A U.S. Navy base in a city in the eastern province of Isla Grande was leased in 1903."

"The sad part of our history, Hassan, is that after Isla Grande became a free country in 1902, until the early part of 1959, we had many turmoils in the different governments. We had always been strongly opposed to dictatorships. Some democratically elected officials were removed by the military, who subsequently established a right-wing dictatorship."

"Our last military dictator was repudiated by most of the Isla Grande citizens, and this promoted the influx of individuals who received the support of the Islanders and also of the United States. They came into power and promised a free, honest, democratic government. However, they selected Communism as a system for perpetuating themselves in power. We unknowingly exchanged a dictatorship from the right to one of the left, which has been disastrous for the Isla Grande people. There are dozens of examples of human rights violations and brutal punishments imposed on individuals who expressed any opposition to the present regime."

"By 1962, there were 40 nuclear missiles in place in Isla Grande which, at that time, were a threat to the United States. The U.S.-Soviet military crisis occurred that same year. The military confrontation ceased through a trade embargo aimed at isolating Isla Grande. The revolutionary government in Isla Grande nationalized American property in 1960 without compensation. Remember, Hassan, Isla Grande was never a third world country."

"In 1961, there was an unsuccessful attempt of over 1,000 Islanders to topple the government. This unsuccessful attempt lasted about three days. Over 1,000 prisoners were allowed to go free in exchange for food and medical supplies."

"There has been more than a 50% drop in the export of agricultural products; a 70% drop of industrial products, and 60% reduction in the gross national product. In 1989, when the Soviet Union supported Isla Grande, 8.2 billion dollars were brought into the island. In 1994, the total was reduced to 1.4 to 1.7 billion dollars."

"Approximately 300 million dollars came from tourism. In 1997, over 520,000 visitors brought in five hundred million dollars. Five hundred million came from the sugar cane industry, 130 million from citric vegetables, and other fruits, about 200 million from minerals, and approximately another 100 million from other sources."

"Lifting of the embargo would provide Fito with the means of obtaining dollars through the International Monetary

Fund and other sources, stimulate investments in Isla Grande, and increase tourism. This will prolong the agony of the Isla Grande people. More than 10% of the Isla Grande population has migrated. In the last years, over 100,000 Islanders have applied for U.S. travel visas. Over 30,000 were rescued from the seas. Most rafters preferred to risk death at sea than to face life in Isla Grande."

"We have always had the ingredients of a superb society and a marvelous country. We have been blessed with the fact there is proximity to the North, Central, South American, and Caribbean countries. We have been a happy, enthusiastic, productive, successful people who enjoyed liberty and took advantage of the opportunities available in Isla Grande."

"Our three strongest products were sugar, tobacco, and coffee. We have been famous for all three. You must know that our music has been enjoyed all over the world. We also have produced outstanding athletes, who still compete and become prominent in many sports."

"Soon after taking control of the country, Fito requested all weapons to be surrendered, in promise of an everlasting peace. On February 3, 1962, during the Kennedy Administration, the United States imposed a full trade embargo, convinced that Fito was moving rapidly towards the establishment of a totalitarian regime in alliance with the Soviet Union. In addition, Fito had confiscated properties owned by U.S. citizens as well as Islanders. Some believe that the killing of Kennedy in November 1963 was related to Fito's revenge. He also had started supporting revolutions throughout Latin America."

"A continent wide embargo was established at the Ninth Meeting of Consultation of Ministers of Foreign Affairs held in July of 1964. The Organization of American States (OAS) sanctions against Isla Grande remained in force during the early 1970's. Shortly thereafter, several countries such as Chile, Peru, and Argentina decided to unilaterally re-establish relations with Isla Grande in contravention of the OAS sanctions, after failing to convince the OAS to formally end the embargo of the Island."

"In 1974, under President Gerald Ford, an improvement in the relationship with Isla Grande was suggested by Congress. The process was quickly derailed when, in late 1975, Isla Grande produced over 40,000 troops that assisted Angola, therefore supporting the Soviet military. President Ford labeled Fito an "international outlaw.""

"In 1976, under President Jimmy Carter, another attempt was made by the United States to improve relations with Isla Grande. In 1977, the "Interest" Section in the Swiss Embassy of the capital was established by the United States, and a similar "Interest" Section in the Czech Embassy in Washington. President Carter relaxed the restrictions of travel by U.S. citizens to the Island. However, in 1978, Fito sent approximately 15,000 troops to Ethiopia and increased his military involvement in Africa, as well as exporting guerillas, training them for Central America."

"From 1975 to 1980, about 300,000 Isla Grande soldiers fought in Angola. Then they were faced with the disaster of 1980: a Boat Lift. One hundred and twenty-five thousand Islanders left the island through the port of El Mar destined for the U.S.A. Among them were spies, criminals, thieves, mentally and physically ill Islanders, and a very large significant group of other undesirables. Fito forced every boat that came to pick up relatives, to board specific people whom he selected. Over 2700 boats left from the Florida Keys. This resulted in a considerable burden to Florida's economy, as well as an increase in social delinquency. Thousands of these "Bad

Islanders" were imprisoned due to repetition of crimes in the United States."

"Under President Reagan, the United States government again enforced the embargo legislation. U.S. businesses were prohibited from dealing with a list of foreign firms operating in the U.S., Panama, and Jamaica, designated as "Isla Grande's fronts, intended to break the U.S. embargo." Also, in 1982, the U.S. government re-imposed the partial ban on travel by its citizens to Isla Grande."

"Finally, Hassan, in 1991, a Bill was passed by Congress. This bipartisan Isla Grande Democracy Act became law, under Present Bush, in October 1992. This law, which received the strong backing of the democratic president, Bill Clinton, strengthened the U.S. embargo against Isla Grande by closing loopholes that allowed foreign subsidiaries of the United States to conduct $700,000,000 a year trade with Isla Grande. The intent of this new law was to bring foreign subsidiary trade with Isla Grande in line with the existing U.S. embargo against countries such as North Korea, Libya, and Iraq."

"The Isla Grande Democracy Act further isolates the Fito regime in the hopes that, eventually, internal revolts will occur and will precipitate either his demise or his departure from the island."

"All of us thought that the loss of Soviet support would become a significant turning point in the history of Isla Grande. In over three decades, it is estimated that Fito's regime received between 100 and 150 billion dollars in Soviet and Eastern European aid, as well as about 1.2 billion dollars a year in military assistance. The Isla Grande military force is the strongest in Latin America. Here you have an island, of a little over ten million people, with a military force that matches countries having three, four, and five times over that of Isla Grande's population.

"The embargo has not been the only one established by the United States, but also one mandated by Fito on his own people. Not even China has such severe repressive force. Rationing has existed for 46 years. In Isla Grande it is a crime to obtain food from farmers. An Islander cannot hire or be hired by another or distribute the product that he or she produces."

"Fito's internal embargo on the freedom and creative forces of the Isla Grande people has worsened the economical crisis and impoverished the people of Isla Grande.

The basis of all this, Hassan, is Fito's lust for international power. His anti-Americanism and his continued warnings about the imminence of an American invasion are meant to distract the public and keep their minds away from their personal problems. These are bits of drama to keep the revolutionary spirit alive."

"His involvement with countries in America, Europe, and Africa is not only for the purpose of international recognition, but also as a lucrative business—he is paid for every Isla Grande person who is sent to fight elsewhere or work in other countries."

"The international community has repeatedly condemned Isla Grande's atrocious human rights record at the United Nations Commission on Human Rights. He has refused inspection of the prisons. Visits to the island by inspectors have been severely curtailed."

"Radio Marti was created by the United Congress in 1983 and has been administered by the United States Information Agency. Twenty-four hours of news and information has been available to Islanders. Only through this and other radio stations, by word of mouth from visitors to the island, and from comments made by Islanders who return after visiting other countries, do the Islanders know about the beautiful opportunities and living conditions that exist elsewhere."

"The current exodus of Islanders was preceded by military desertions. In one week in 1993, two Isla Grande Air Force MIGS defected. Commercial airlines were also diverted to Florida. The Isla Grande black market flourishes."

"Hassan, it is estimated that no less than 12,500 executions have occurred under Fito's regime. Over two million people have requested exile. Fito manifests symptoms of paranoia in the constant turnover of personnel, jailing, and physically eliminating his closest friends. He conducted a single party election in February of 1993; a sham, as the election precluded the inclusion of candidates not sanctioned by the Communist Party."

"Confrontations constantly occur throughout the island. We only became aware of a few of them. Nevertheless, Fito has survived the administration of ten U.S. Presidents and has been responsible for one of the longest dictatorships in the history of the world."

"The tragedy that we are all seeing must reach an end. No human being should be allowed to enslave their fellow countrymen and impose their will indefinitely. Hassan, you can help yourself and millions of Islanders. Listen carefully."

"I shall," Hassan answered.

"I am going to propose a project for which you will be paid two million dollars," Alex said. "It will be very simple for you to execute. First, you must return to Isla Grande and visit Ricardo, Fito's brother. You will bring with you the drawings of a very sophisticated boat that we will call Blackshark."

He then showed pictures and drawings, and gave them to Hassan with explicit literature. "You must read the specifications of Blackshark and leave these drawings and specs for Ricardo to review. You can tell him that Isla Grande can receive it as a gift! This means the Islanders will not pay the two and a half million dollars, the cost of Blackshark. Even if they wanted to buy it, this would be impossible."

"The gift is to be received by Fito on the afternoon of July 28. If Ricardo accepts the gift, you must then return to Miami and negotiate with the Mag Company for the construction and delivery of Blackshark, before next July 1. During the period of construction, you will return to Miami periodically, and bring with you three of Fito's closest assistants, who will be trained in all aspects of the operation of Blackshark and its weapons.

"At the time of writing of the contract with the Mag Company, you must bring half a million dollars for the down payment. You will not be obligated to pay the balance of two million dollars. I will explain later why."

"Upon the completion of the construction of the boat, sea trials will take place, first around Miami, and the last one in Key West. The last sea trial must be held July 28. I will tell you later what you and your Isla Grande friends must do with the boat."

"When the boat reaches Isla Grande (as an "extension" of the sea trial in Key West) you will receive two million dollars wherever you designate us to deliver the money. The money will be in an escrow account and the custodian of these two million dollars will have instructions that, upon a telephone call from me, the monies will be delivered immediately to you. On July 28, you will be in Florida and from Key West you must fly to the Bahamas where you will be contacted. Under no circumstances should it be known that you and I have had this discussion."

Hassan asked Alex about his background and motivation. Alex replied that since the assassination of his wife, he decided to devote the rest of his days to the cause of freedom and that he was blessed by a successful professional practice.

"Hassan replied, "Alex, I like you. I respect idealism, honesty and integrity. You seem to have these and many other good qualities. I have indicated that I would like to "retire" comfortably with Eva, my assistant, in a haven such as the Bahamas. Your request sounds reasonable and I will carry out your instructions as you have stated. Tomorrow I will return to Isla Grande via Mexico. As soon as I convince the Isla Grande government to accept this gift, I will return to Miami and will see you again."

They shook hands, and the following morning, Hassan flew to Isla Grande.

CHAPTER 10

MEETING OF THE COUNCIL
OF ISLA GRANDE'S AFFAIRS IN MIAMI

As previously stated, Alex was a successful, well-known physician and businessman. He had been married to Lucia, Fito's sister. Soon after the revolution brought Fito into power, Lucia threatened to publicly denounce the true motivations of her brother. Fito then poisoned her to death and she was found dead on a lake close to the private beach section of the capital of the country. Alex was about to be detained but successfully fled to the United States. Once there, Alex, who was very talented and a hard-working man, developed several profitable businesses. He suspected that his wife's death was Fito's doing and bore a deep hatred for him and his "full of lies" regime.

Alex called a meeting of twelve Isla Grande refugees who were his closest friends. They shared the commonality of being financially successful and were prominent naturalized

American citizens, all interested in the freedom of Isla Grande. The group consisted of highly intelligent, mature, mostly middle-aged, and a few elderly individuals.

Alex had called the meeting to illustrate the fruitless efforts of the Islander exiles in trying to promote changes in Isla Grande and to present his ingenious plan and make a request of the group. They met in the Boardroom of a private club in Miami. Alex sat at the head of the U-shaped table. Opposite the table were a large TV screen and a CD player operated by Alex. Only the twelve Islander exiles, including Alex, were present. He turned on the VCR and TV and showed a series of video clips that illustrated the tragedy of the rafters.

"Note this empty boat that is drifting close to the coast of Florida," he said.

"Its passengers drowned." He continued, "Now, note this primitive vessel. It was built from the roof of a bus and used an improvised small, single sail. Believe it or not, its occupants were spotted and arrived safely to the coast of Florida.

"Now, this is the body of one of the many who never made it. These are human extremities floating on the water. They belonged to a rafter who was attacked and partially eaten by sharks. This next scene shows a teenager who recently survived after receiving the only life jacket available. The youngster suffered the emotional trauma of observing his parents drown. He has been left with permanent emotional scars."

The video progressed, displaying images of several ships.

These are ships from Mexico, Canada, Russia, and South American countries," he said. "They have delivered goods to Isla Grande and taken goods from Isla Grande to other countries. We know of many dock strikes triggered by the Isla Grande government exporting food at a time when its citizens were starving. The resentment of the stevedores was well justified. Can you imagine being hungry and forced to load meat and many other products onto Russian ships?"

"Many pieces of treasured artwork also have been sent to Russia. The famous metal lions that adorned the Paseo del Prado, those unique, famous sculptures, were given to Russia. I have seen in the Hermitage Museum in St. Petersburg thousands of artworks that the Czars imported from all over the world. The Communists have continued this similar custom and have obtained valuable pieces of art from many countries that were obligated to them. God knows where the Isla Grande lions now reside."

"Fito has purchased goods from Latin American countries and from Europe. Many of these goods were acquired in exchange for products of Isla Grande. His most needed commodity has been fuel. He has been selling properties, businesses, and any desirable land to foreign countries in exchange for dollars. He has benefited personally from these transactions. We have documentation of all activities related to his personal bank savings accounts in Europe and Asia."

"The biggest failure of Isla Grande's revolution has been the steady decrease in the harvest of sugar cane. In 1994, it dropped to four hundred million dollars; the lowest amount in the history of Isla Grande. A drop in price on the world market, low productivity due to poor exploitation of the sugar cane fields, and the lack of workers' incentives have provoked this crisis. Equipment in sugar mills and in factories is outdated. Equipment imported from Europe, and particularly, Russia, has been of poor quality. There has been a scarcity of technological help. Many factories and businesses have been shut down because of lack of parts and equipment. Fito has sent Islanders to be trained abroad. Many of the Islanders remained abroad and requested political asylum. Those who returned generally were not of the same integrity as the Islanders who fled the island in the 60's."

"The arrival of goods from different parts of the world has made the so-called blockade ineffective."

He then showed scenes of exile groups in military training in the Everglades, and said, "Some groups of naturalized Americans have practiced and have mastered the use of weapons. If time and circumstances permit, they could be the nucleus of the military force that would fight for Isla Grande's freedom."

"Isla Grande has the largest army in Latin America, over 150,000 well-trained soldiers. We never expected another country to fight for us. We have been disappointed that no country, since the time of Kennedy, has allowed the exiles to organize as a military force, travel to Isla Grande and establish an effective underground force. Some efforts to move military personnel to Isla Grande have been averted by the U.S. Coast Guard."

He then showed the debates in the Human Rights Committee of the United Nations and in Geneva, Switzerland. "We have presented many documents demonstrating the atrocities of the Isla Grande government and the testimony of hundreds of ex-prisoners who have related the inhumane treatment of prisoners," Alex said. "Thousands have been serving jail sentences because they expressed their aversion to the way the country was being governed. International organizations have been requested to send observers. However, Fito has prohibited any inspection of the jails where unmerciful punishment occurs daily."

He then showed shots of exile groups parading in front of the White House, around Capital Hill, and in Miami. "We have established offices in Washington to lobby with members of both Democratic and Republican parties," he said. "We have supported any congressman who advances the cause of freedom and, particularly, Isla Grande. Thanks to them the embargo of Isla Grande has been reinforced."

"However, we have been unsuccessful in trying to expand the economic blockade. A total blockade would keep Fito's enemies, the rafters, on the island. I strongly believe that, eventually, there would be an internal revolt. The Armed Forces would be divided into those that would follow Fito's instructions to kill protestors and those that wouldn't. The latter might then join the protestors. Inevitably, Fito would be forced out and would have to leave the island to save himself, or he would be killed."

He then showed images of the Isla Grande dictator visiting Spain, Colombia, Brazil, Mexico, Argentina and other countries. "Note the smiles of the leaders of other countries," he said, "who either remain silent or hypocritically converse with the dictator. They fear his government may support guerillas in their own country. They often disagree with him when they meet among themselves, but in his presence, they express affection and admiration. This is another way they manifest their anti-American feelings. The United States is too often blamed for the financial problems of many Latin-American countries."

Alex then showed videos of the fruitless attempts at Fito's assassination in and outside of Isla Grande. "A variety of weapons, explosives, poisons, and many other methods have failed to kill this dictator. In view of all these failures, there is only one thing that will work and that is to implement my plan to physically eliminate him, without hurting innocent people."

Following this statement, the attendants looked at each other with expressions of surprise. With these remarks, Alex concluded the video presentation. The lights went on and Alex proceeded to discuss his plan.

"I have a plan that I call the "Omega Project." Blackshark is the name I have given to the newest, most sophisticated marine vessel ever built, which could be used to destroy the elite of the Isla Grande government. We will 'donate' Blackshark to the Isla Grande government. I do not want to reveal the details of the project now. What I have said today cannot be commented on outside this room. To finance this project, we will need three million dollars. I will contribute the first quarter of a million dollars."

There was a rumbling in the room. Alex then directed his comments to each of the twelve members of the group.

He looked first at Juan. "Juan, you have been very successful in the sugar cane industry. You have plantations in the Dominican Republic which has been the major place of your business. You and your family have lived well in this country and abroad. I thank you for your willingness to continue supporting the cause of freedom in our native country, Isla Grande."

"Carlos, you have made a fortune importing fruits from Central America into this country. You have been signaled by the President of the United States as an example of what hard work, persistence, and good ideas can mean to a person. You have devoted countless hours to the cause of freedom, and I thank you for your collaboration."

"Armando, you have been one of the most successful developers in South Florida. You came to this country as a teenager and lived in a foster home. Your incredible talent first brought you success in the field of computers. In the last decade you have devoted a considerable amount of time to the cause of Isla Grande, and I thank you for being with us."

"Fernando, you have lived part of your life in Isla Grande and part in Puerto Rico. You are living permanently now in Miami, enjoying the product of your efforts. You would have been successful in any country where you lived. You have always been a nonpretentious, successful man and Isla Grande has always been close to your heart. Thanks for being with us."

"Ramon, you have just recently settled in Miami. You retired at a very young age from a very successful business. You have developed shopping centers and control a considerable amount of land in Puerto Rico. You continue your success in South Florida and live quietly here with your beautiful family. Your roots are in Isla Grande and I know you have always helped our cause. We count on you, not only now, but in the future, when Isla Grande becomes free again.

"Jose, you have excelled as a banker. You were the most popular Isla Grande banker and continue doing so. Your American associates have signaled you as one of the very few good things that have happened as a result of Isla Grande's dictatorship. Hundreds of talented Islanders like yourself have become successful in our adopted country. You love the United States, but also love Isla Grande. I thank you for being with us."

"Aurelio, you have struggled probably more than any of us who are sitting around this table. You started from scratch thirty years ago and succeeded in numerous businesses. You semi-retired after investing in properties that are now providing you a steady income. You are a quiet, superb human being, who also would like to help re-establish democracy in Isla Grande. Thanks."

"Leslie, you are a professional gambler in the good sense of the word. You have excelled in the field of insurance and in the stock market. Not only have you helped yourself and your family, but also many friends who needed help to start their own business. You have an incredible number of grateful clients. Your heart and soul are in the United States and in Isla Grande at the same time. Thanks for being with us."

"Dear Mario, you have spent as much time in an airplane as on land. Your international businesses have homes in many parts of the world, but your home in Miami, and, eventually, your home in Isla Grande, will be your favorite spots. Thanks for your continued support."

"Dear Isaac, you belong to an illustrious family of perennial immigrants. Your family went from Europe to America and then from Isla Grande to the United States. You have continued your successful manufacturing business and have established many factories in Miami. I am sure you will create a similar business in free Isla Grande. Thanks for your support."

"Jorge, you started in this country as a salesman and have developed a drug empire. By drugs I mean pharmaceuticals and not addictive drugs, naturally. (Everyone laughed). I know you are ready to supply, on short notice, medicines and other goods to a free Isla Grande and would like to offer your talent in the restructuring of the new, free Isla Grande society. Thanks for your collaboration."

Alex then addressed the group. "Jose, as the banker and oldest of the group, I would like you to become the treasurer and the custodian of the funds. These funds must become available when the mission is successfully completed. We will all give the checks for you to deposit. Two checks, one for a million dollars and another for two million will be paid to the executors of the project, only if the project becomes successful. If, for some reason, the project fails, each of our contribution will be returned."

"My plan is probably the last effort to topple the dictatorship; this is the reason I call my project the Omega Project, Omega being the last letter of the Greek Alphabet."

Upon completion of Alex' presentation, they all joined in touching their hands on the table and, Jose, the oldest of the group, thanked Alex and encouraged him to proceed immediately with the implementation of the Omega Project.

CHAPTER 11

HASSAN IN ISLA GRANDE

After the meeting with Alex, Hassan returned to Isla Grande and asked for a meeting with Ricardo. He met with him in Colonia, the headquarters of the Isla Grande Armed Forces. The largest battalion of servicemen is based at this installation located in the outskirts of the capital. When Fito visited Colonia, all servicemen were requested to dispose of their weapons which were placed in a special room, guarded by members of Fito's private army. Only Fito's personal guard had weapons when he visited Colonia. After the military parade, the members of the Armed Forces were allowed to regain their weapons.

Ricardo received Hassan at his office. Different from Fito's office, Ricardo had a plain desk with neatly arranged files and papers. The décor was simple. There was a sofa and a few chairs. The only interesting wall was one that had weapons that dealt from the time of the Spanish War to present date. Old and modern rifles, guns, and machine guns were on display on the wall to the right of the desk. Ricardo asked Hassan to sit in front of him. Hassan met Ricardo and explained his plan. "Ricardo, I can provide you with the most sophisticated vessel ever built which you will use for patrolling your coasts. Your government will save fuel by eliminating several obsolete coast guard patrol vessels. I can do this at no cost to your government! I've called it Blackshark. Isla Grande would never be able to buy this vessel because it is built in the United States and only sold to friendly countries with which they have diplomatic relations. It would please Fito if you presented him with the gift of this boat next July 28, when you celebrate another anniversary of the revolution. You should surprise him with this gift. We can all join and celebrate with Fito on the Presidential Yacht and show him the remarkable features of this vessel."

"Please tell me more about Blackshark," Ricardo said.

"This vessel has the ability to accurately destroy a target while cruising at 40 miles per hour, regardless of rough seas," Hassan explained.

"Electronic equipment is available on board with sophisticated computers that allow a cannon to aim accurately upon identifying the target. Infrared technology and lasers permit performance of this task during the day and also at night. The engines operate virtually silently. Machine guns on board can annihilate enemy aircraft."

"This vessel could patrol your coast at high speed consuming relatively small amounts of diesel fuel. This vessel has been sold to some Arab countries and, pretending I am a Saudi diplomat, I can acquire it on the pretext of using it for patrolling the coasts of Saudi Arabia. Obviously, the vessel will never get to Saudi Arabia. It will be hijacked to Isla Grande from the United States by three of your best and loyal men that you will select for this mission."

"Fito will be delighted with the show we can put on with Blackshark. Blackshark, under the control of your selected crewmen, will perform at a distance from the Presidential Yacht in Valero. It will blow up a small vessel and knock down a flying object. You must arrange for these targets to become available and be launched from one of your patrol boats on the afternoon of July 28. We will have a ball and the most important thing is that it will cost you nothing! In exchange for this two and a half million dollar gift, I want you to donate to me some art work I have seen in some of the confiscated homes we have visited. Later I'll give you the list and the addresses. This art work should be delivered to the Alcanian Embassy."

"You will have no problem with the United States, because, as I said, I'll buy Blackshark on the pretext it will go to Saudi Arabia," Hassan continued. "Three of your most loyal men will join me in Miami and will be disguised as Saudi officers. They will be trained in all aspects of the operation of Blackshark and its weapons. The vessel will be built and tested by next July 1. The final sea trial will be held on July 28. On this day, Blackshark will be hijacked."

"Following the hijacking of Blackshark by your men, I will leave Miami, never to return to the United States. The balance of the payment of this vessel (which will cost a total of two and one-half million dollars) will not be claimed to Isla Grande because it will not be purchased by the Isla Grande government! As soon as you get the boat, you will repaint and disguise it and use it for patrolling your coast."

"How will you pay for Blackshark? Our country is broke!" Ricardo asked.

"You don't have to come up with hard cash," Hassan replied. "In order to acquire the vessel, I must provide half a million dollars at the time of signing the contract. I will give you a copy of the contract and a copy of the check given to the Mag Corporation. I will only need from you half a million dollars in cash for the deposit."

"How can I come up with this money?" Ricardo asked.

"Easily. I will bring drugs from Europe for you to convert into hard currency. We have access to hard drugs from Turkey. In the next 48 hours, a ship from Alcania will arrive in Isla Grande with the drugs," Hassan continued.

"In addition to the cash, you must assign your three best men to this project. I will take them to Miami with me and pretend that they are officers from Saudi Arabia. They will be trained by Mag Company to operate the vessel and to familiarize themselves with the weapons on board Blackshark. When Blackshark completes its last sea trial on July 28 in the Florida Keys, your three men will seize the vessel. We should spare the lives of the three Americans on board. We want no problems with the United States government. Later, they will be safely returned to the United States. Our men will tell the American crew members they are from Arabia and that the boat is going to Isla Grande, and from there, to an Arab country. This will prevent the Isla Grande government from being blamed for the theft of the vessel. Obviously, the balance of the payment to the Mag Company will never be made. Ricardo, think about this and let me know your reaction at your earliest convenience."

CHAPTER 12

HASSAN AT HIS HOME

Hassan left Colonia and returned to his beautiful home in the country club district. Private homes of wealthy Islanders were confiscated by the Isla Grande government and many were given to diplomats. Eva was waiting for him, wearing a small bikini. She hugged Hassan and they kissed. Hassan walked slowly to his bedroom, followed by Eva. He put on his bathing suit and walked down to the swimming pool with Eva. While by the pool, he talked to her.

"Eva, we've been together for a number of years. You wanted to see America and we were assigned to Isla Grande. Undoubtedly this is a beautiful island, but we cannot enjoy its beauty because of what has happened to its people. I have plans to take you on a long journey. I have noticed that you have been watched closely by Fito and some of his assistants. I want you to be careful with these Islanders who show very little respect for women."

"Hassan, don't worry," Eva replied. "As a blonde woman, I am more noticeable among the beautiful Isla Grande women whom I have seen. No one will take me away from you. I must tell you that I have caught you many times looking at these beautiful brunettes. I have been watching you! Are you interested in any of them?"

"We both have flirting eyes that are not exclusive for each other. We both enjoy watching beautiful people and things," Hassan answered. "We may have temptations, but I can assure you that no one has ever tempted me here, or anywhere else. I fully enjoy your company, your support, and your help."

"When I leave you for a few days, I miss you very much. I must leave you soon again. You can rest assured that you are always in my heart. In a few days, I may have to go back to Mexico to finalize a deal. I expect it will take me only three days. This time I must go alone. Be patient, because I expect that a lot of good things will happen to us as a result of this deal."

Eva kissed Hassan and both dove into the swimming pool.

Two days later, Hassan, while sunbathing by the pool of his luxurious mansion with the lovely Eva, received a telephone call from Ricardo.

"Hassan, your plan appears foolproof. I have consulted with Ivan, the leader of Fito's personal guard, and he has agreed to go with two loyal assistants and you to Miami. If for no other reason, he wants to visit the United States for the first time! I will get you the money as soon as you deliver the goods."

A ship from Turkey arrived two days later. Cocaine and hashish were part of the cargo. It was delivered to Ricardo who passed it on to Colombian dealers. They gave Ricardo five million dollars. Three days later, Hassan received a black briefcase containing half a million dollars in cash.

It is important to note that the ideal geographic location of Isla Grande facilitated an intermediate stop of vessels carrying hard drugs coming from Asia, Europe and South America (particularly from Colombia).

The drug business was controlled by some high ranking officers from Isla Grande's Armed Forces.

The drugs were subsequently smuggled to the US usually on cargo ships. Many ingenious techniques have been used to bring drugs to the United States. One has been stuffed cadavers with cocaine. Another has been dolls and toys filled with cocaine. Mules are willing people who volunteer to swallow cocaine-filled condoms. They bring a load of cocaine in the stomach and bowel. Many have died from the rupture of some of the condoms which cause irreversible neurological complications that lead to death.

CHAPTER 13

HASSAN IN MIAMI

The following day, Hassan flew to Mexico City and from there to Miami. Hassan visited the owner of the Mag Company and discussed the purchase of a patrol vessel for Saudi Arabia. After many hours and two days of discussion, they consummated the deal.

Hassan said, "Here is the half million dollar deposit for Blackshark which you'll build. It must go to Saudi Arabia next July and must meet the specifications outlined in the contract. The balance of two million dollars will be paid upon delivery of Blackshark. I have put in the contract that if you cannot deliver Blackshark by next July 1, you will return my deposit and will pay a penalty of $100,000. I will take care of securing the necessary U.S. export licenses for the boat, armaments and electronics systems. You will have the necessary papers before the boat is ready for delivery. Your experts at Mag Company must teach the three people that I will bring with me all the details of the operation of Blackshark. I will visit with you periodically and follow the progress of the construction of Blackshark." A few minutes later, a bottle of champagne was opened and the deal was closed.

The Mag Company had built these unique patrol boats for several countries in the Middle East and also sold them to the US Navy. This is the only company in the World that builds fast boats housing a variety of sophisticated weaponry.

The President of the Mag Company was unaware that several features would be added to Blackshark, such as the reinforced hull and deck, as well as magnetic repelling devices along the sides of the boat. Other devices such as the smoke forming instruments and the bullet proof helmet would be added at a later date.

Hassan was delighted with his visit to the Mag Company. He telephoned Alex and they met at a private club not too far from the Mag Company.

Hassan spoke, "Alex, we will have the vessel ready for the sea trial in the next couple of weeks. The final sea trial will take place in July. It is my intention to bring to Miami three important gentlemen who will learn all the features of the vessel. I will stay with them at a hotel close to the airport. I must watch the behavior of one of these three individuals. He is poorly educated, quite aggressive, and very impatient. This will be the first trip of the three to Miami. I will make sure that we have no problems while these three are in Miami.

Alex replied, "Hassan, you have done a marvelous job. I hope I never meet your "friends." Make sure that they don't get in trouble. There are many temptations in Miami. Avoid the night spots in Miami Beach and get them tired by touring very interesting spots, such as the Seaquarium, the Everglades National Park, the Viscaya Castle, and other attractive sites.

They shook hands and Alex returned to his practice.

CHAPTER 14

THE TESTING OF BLACKSHARK

Hassan periodically visited the Mag Company and secretly met with Alex. He carefully followed all steps pertaining to the construction of Blackshark. In late May, while in the capital of Isla Grande, he was informed that Blackshark would soon be ready for testing. He immediately called Ricardo and asked for the three men he had previously mentioned. Hassan said that the following morning, the three men would fly with him to Miami, via Mexico, and visit the Mag Company for inspection and testing of Blackshark. The testing would take place on Wednesday.

Hassan met Ivan for the first time at Colonia, the military headquarters. Ivan was a husky, ruthless Isla Grande official, who had enjoyed all the privileges of those who worked closest to Fito. He received his military training in Russia and had served several tours of duty in Iraq and in Angola. He was the leader of the militia that attacked a group of dissidents in the area where Simon's father was injured. The other two men, Quico and Miguel, were from Isla Grande's Navy and were handpicked by Ivan. Ivan and his two assistants met with Hassan. Quico and Miguel looked like brothers. Both were short, muscular, and looked tough. Quico was senior to Miguel after spending many more years in the Navy.

Hassan said, "Ivan, the four of us will go to Miami to visit the Mag Company. You will see the most sophisticated vessel ever built."

The following morning, Hassan, Ivan, and his assistants flew to Mexico City, and from there to Miami. They stayed at a hotel close to the airport. They came to Miami on the pretext that they were members of the Saudi Arabian Army and had come to Florida on a business mission. That evening, Ivan went partying with Quico and Miguel. At the nearby bar, Ivan had too many drinks and there was a brief altercation with the bartender. Quico and Miguel took Ivan back to the hotel and the following morning they were picked up by Hassan and the four went to the Mag Company.

On Wednesday morning they arrived at the Mag Company. As soon as Simon saw Ivan, he remembered him from his days in Isla Grande. Ivan didn't recognize Simon, who had grown a beard and a mustache. Simon made no comment. Ivan spoke English with a Hispanic accent.

That same morning, Blackshark was launched. Simon, his brother, Tony, and Everett, a weaponry expert and employee of the Mag Company, and Ivan and his two assistants boarded the vessel. They cruised the waters off the coast of Miami Beach.

The visitors were impressed with the maneuverability and the stability of the vessel. Simon aimed a gun at a vessel that was seen at a far distance. Ivan observed on the television screen that the target remained in sharp focus despite the up and down motion of the vessel.

Simon then turned the vessel towards the beach. They focused the telescope on bikini-clad girls. Ivan was delighted with the beautiful body of a bather and shouted with excitement "Bravo!"

Simon's brother showed Miguel, one of Ivan's assistants, how to operate the machine gun.

That Wednesday night, they took Blackshark out to show Ivan and his assistants the operation of the vessel using infrared detectors and infrared light. The Islanders were delightfully pleased. The following day they returned with Hassan to Isla Grande via Mexico. On Friday, Ivan described to Ricardo their experience with Blackshark.

Ricardo was enthused. He was unaware of the existence of such a vessel. Blackshark would fill in the deficiencies of Isla Grande's naval forces. One such vessel would replace several of their patrol boats. The citizens who planned an escape from the Island would learn that, if their primitive vessels would be detected by Blackshark patrol crew, they would be destroyed. It would also lend great prestige to Isla Grande to possess such a boat.

CHAPTER 15

THE ESCAPE OF LIDIA AND MARIO

During the early hours of July 27, there was a farewell meeting which included Lidia's parents and Mario's mother. Lidia's mother spoke openly. "Lidia, you've always been a stubborn girl. I've failed to talk you out of this crazy trip. My heart has shrunken from sorrow. I don't know if I'll ever see you again!" Tears ran over her wrinkled, pale cheeks. Lidia's mother continued, "The only present I can give you is this necklace which has two charms. One is the Virgin of Charity, who, as you know, has performed many miracles and has saved many fishermen. That is why she is depicted with a boat and three fishermen at her feet. She will protect you both on your journey. The second charm is this little, multifaceted sphere. When sun strikes this sphere, the colors of the rainbow are displayed. This sphere will portray light and beauty at all times; it symbolizes life. I have always worn this charm close to my heart. Now it is yours. Wear it always."

Lidia did not know how valuable this charm would turn out to be. Mario's parents remained silent. They suppressed their feelings of anguish. They hugged each other and cried. Mario and Lidia said good-bye and walked out of the small house into the bushes to retrieve **Cucaracha**. The two, plus Mario's parents and Lidia's mother, dragged the small vessel to a solitary nearby beach. They had collected several jars of water, several loaves of bread, a block of guava, fruits and two hats.

Mario and Lidia wore long-sleeved shirts and hats. Lidia placed the necklace around her neck. They boarded the small boat and started rowing. Their parents returned to their homes, not wanting to be spotted waving and crying on the beach at the same time. Mario rowed out of the protected beach area. He raised an improvised sail. The early part of the trip was uneventful. When Mario and Lidia were about five miles off the coast, the wind suddenly changed to an east and then to a northeast direction. The prevailing winds during the summer months in the Caribbean are from the southeast. This and the five knot south-to-north course of the Gulfstream help the cruise of vessels towards the Florida coast. When the wind comes from the north or northeast, they oppose the direction of the Gulf stream which is south to north. Lidia and Mario soon encountered four to six foot waves. This made rowing and sailing an arduous task. Twelve hours into their journey, they were just about fifteen miles from the coast of Isla Grande.

From several cities of the United States, Miami, Fort Lauderdale, New Orleans etc, cruise ships constantly sail to several Caribbean Islands, Central America, and South America. Many rafters have indicated great frustration when in their journey to the US they see at the distance beautiful cruise ships which do not became aware of their needs.

The rafters have thoughts such as, "it is very frustrating to imagine thousands of people, dining, wining and being entertained in the safety of a luxurious moving hotel and casino, while we are freezing, starving and greatly concerned if we are ever going to make it out of this ordeal alive."

Many rafters run out of food and water. Many have seen how some drink salt water in desperation, quickly deteriorating and eventually drowning.

Rafts are often surrounded by sharks. It is of interest to note that when dolphins appear, the sharks seem to swim away. It has been stated that sharks are cautious with dolphins, who can strike the shark's back head-on and crack their spines.

There are stories where dolphins have surrounded small vessels and accompanied the vessel close to the coast of the Florida Keys. Dolphins are the best companions of the rafters.

Dehydration and sunburn are the rafters' worst enemies.

The most frustrating experiences are to see large cruise ships and fishing boats from a distance, which course oblivious to the ordeals of the rafters. Some of the rafts capsize early in their journey. The poor construction of many rafts accounts for the drowning of hundreds of rafters. The marine conditions in the Gulfstream can change within six hours. One can see a bright sunny day be followed by high seas and winds that change from the southeast to the west, and sometimes northwest and north. When north winds appear, high waves follow. This is because the Gulfstream runs from south to north, opposite the direction of the winds when they come from the north or northwest. When cruising the Caribbean, one should get weather reports and only count on them for the following six hours.

While alone in the middle of the ocean, many thoughts come to the minds of the rafters. They all risk their lives with the goal of obtaining freedom. Freedom is the driving force. Religious feelings strengthen the determination and mitigate the thirst and hunger. Lidia had not imagined the feeling of loneliness, particularly during the evening. Fortunately she was not prone to seasickness. She became drowsy, and only after midnight, Lidia and Mario would fall asleep. A beautiful sunset would be followed by pitch dark night. Sunsets are prettier than dawn. They last longer; the sky is full of colors. The scenery that one observes will never be repeated. The enjoyment of the sunset should be experienced by every human being.

Sunrise came too fast. The rafters were eager to see vessels around **Cucharacha.** They were hungry and thirsty but, at the same time, extremely optimistic.

They could not imagine what they would be subjected to during the next 24 hours.

CHAPTER 16

THE FINAL SEA TRIAL OF BLACKSHARK

On July 24, Hassan, Ivan, Quico, and Miguel flew to Mexico and then to Miami, arriving in the afternoon of July 24. Hassan went alone to the Mag Company and checked the schedule for the final testing. They planned the final sea trial on July 28.

If successful, they promised to accept delivery of the boat the following week and produce its final payment. The plans were for Hassan to drive with Quico and Miguel to Key West. Ivan would remain in Miami and would join the American crewmen for the trip to Key West on Blackshark.

Ivan remained in Miami alone. That evening he almost got into a fracas at a local bar. This had happened before. As he knew of his great responsibility, he finally controlled himself. The following morning he arrived early at the Mag Company.

On the evening of July 27, Simon had informed Alex they were going to carry out the last sea trial in the early morning of July 28.

Alex met Simon privately at Alex's home. They discussed Phase 2 of the Omega project which would begin in Key West.

On July 28 of 1953, Fito and 110 revolutionaries had attacked the Montada barracks in the Eastern Province. Fito was captured, tried, imprisoned, and finally released, only to regroup in Mexico. In 1956, he returned from Mexico with 81 men in a 43 foot boat. Within two years he rode in triumph into Isla Grande's capital, Valencia. Every year thereafter, a big celebration took place on July 28.

"I'm very excited," Simon said. "July 28 is the day that I have been waiting for." Alex explained Phase 3 of the operation. He said, "I know we will succeed. We will contact you as soon as I return to Key West."

Simon was unaware of the unexpected turn of events that would subsequently take place.

Early on the morning of July 28, Simon, his brother, and Everett boarded Blackshark. They informed the Mag Company of the plan, which was to conduct a final sea trial, with emphasis on the study of fuel consumption and long-range cruising. They were to make a run from Miami to Key West (160 miles) and back to Miami, on the same day. Ivan joined them.

They left at sunrise. They reached Key West in four hours on a non-stop trip. They arrived before noon and docked at a fuel station. A Coast Guard vessel approached Blackshark and questioned them about their mission. Simon identified himself and his crew and replied that they were on a final sea trial and would be heading back to Miami that afternoon.

Quico, Miguel, and Hassan traveled to Key West on July 27. On July 28 they planned to board the three Islanders on Blackshark and later to hijack the vessel to Isla Grande. Quico and Miguel boarded Blackshark at the fuel dock on the pretext that they wanted a "free ride" back to Miami with Ivan. The six passengers on Blackshark left the marina at 12:15 p.m. Simon was at the helm of the vessel. Hassan returned to Miami by plane, and from there he flew to Nassau, Bahamas. At a distance he saw Blackshark cruising off the coast. Little did Hassan know about the true mission of Blackshark and its final destination.

CHAPTER 17

THE SEIZING OF BLACKSHARK

About two miles off the coast of Key West, Ivan and his assistants pulled out guns and seized the vessel. Simon, Tony, and Everett offered no resistance and were bound. Ivan said to the three, "Don't be afraid; you won't be killed . . . . yet. We are taking this vessel to Isla Grande; later it will go to Saudi Arabia. I am just going to have some fun with it! You'll be returned later to the United States." Ivan thought that Simon, Tony, and Everett were convinced they were Arab officials and not Fito's agents.

Simon looked at Ivan with anger and despair. He and his friends tried desperately to free themselves, regain control of the vessel, and carry out the second phase of the Omega Project.

The original plan was to get close to Isla Grande with Blackshark and drop Ivan and his friends in the ocean; next they would try to destroy Fito's boat.

Simon, Tony and Everett became very frustrated and thought that they would be killed or put in jail and that Blackshark would end up in Isla Grande, not in Saudi Arabia.

During the hours that it took from Key West to the northern coast of Isla Grande, Ivan took pleasure in describing his adventures in countries such as Angola in Africa. He asked Quico and Miguel, "Do we have any beer? We must celebrate very soon."

They had an Igloo cooler and the three enjoyed the pleasure of cold beers. Simon, Everett, and Peter were tied and placed in the cockpit. The deck was left for Ivan, Quico, and Miguel. Little did Ivan know that Simon, Peter, and Everett were prepared for such an event. Each had hidden knives in their shoes. Although they could not cut their own ropes, they could cut the ropes of each other by turning on their sides. All this took place quite easily because Ivan, Quico, and Miguel paid no attention to the three who were in the cockpit.

Simon looked at Peter and Everett and asked that they pretend that they were tied until the right moment would arise. The plans were to jump Ivan, Quico, and Miguel while they were distracted at the sight of the northern coast of Isla Grande. The only thing to do at that time was to wait.

CHAPTER 18

ENCOUNTERING ROUGH SEAS
AND SPOTTING CUCARACHA

Ivan's plan was to cruise at an average of 40 mph and arrive close to Valero Beach by no later than 4 p.m. At that time, the "show" would start; Blackshark would perform for Fito and his entourage. Ricardo had made the necessary arrangements.

Since late morning on July 28, the wind persisted blowing from the northeast and built rough seas. Suddenly, about 20 miles off the northern coast of Isla Grande, the passengers of Blackshark saw a small boat with its two lonely passengers on board. Ivan, who was at the helm, said, "Quico, practice target shooting with the machine gun." Quico answered, "OK, boss." He aimed the gun at **Cucaracha** with the laser and fired a round expecting to kill its two passengers and sink the boat. As bullets whistled over Lidia and Mario's heads, they jumped into the ocean. **Cucaracha** drifted away from them unharmed. Lidia and Mario remained drifting for a while and later swam unsuccessfully toward **Cucaracha**. They could not understand why a black vessel would shoot at them. They were unaware of any black Coast Guard vessel from Isla Grande.

"I believe I made a hit. Can we check?" Quico asked.

"Let's forget this," Ivan responded. We have no time to waste. We are pressed for time. We'll continue at top speed to our final destination. There are more important things to do." They believed that Lidia and Mario had been killed and that the **Cucaracha** sank.

Simon looked from the cockpit at Ivan and cursed him for what he had just done. He well remembered Ivan's viciousness and his sarcastic face, from his days in Isla Grande. Ivan entered the cockpit and slapped Simon's face. He had no idea what was coming to him. He was unaware that Simon, Everett, and Peter were no longer restrained.

Blackshark continued its race toward Isla Grande.

Lidia and Mario hopelessly struggled to recover **Cucaracha**. The rough seas made it impossible for them to get close to the boat. With a feeling of relief, they saw at a distance Blackshark heading away from them. They had feared that Blackshark would turn around and that's why they didn't try initially to reach the **Cucaracha**. Fortunately, both were wearing life jackets and, most importantly, they never lost their faith.

Mario said to Lidia, "Don't struggle in the ocean. We should behave like the fishes, which means to swim slowly towards **Cucaracha**. Don't be afraid. I am swimming next to you and if I see a shark, I will put myself between the shark and you.

Lidia replied, "I am certainly not afraid when I have you next to me. I sometimes wonder if this was a good idea. It is too late to become pessimistic. I know that I have too many people praying that we will make it. The Lord has always been with me and will not let us down."

CHAPTER 19

THE CELEBRATION OF THE 28TH OF JULY
AND THE "SURPRISE" PARTY

On the 28th of July throughout the country, there were many celebrations. Although thousands of islanders were unhappy with their lives, they were told to take off from work and enjoy the music and dancing which were offered usually at small parks in every village and in major cities.

Prior to getting into Valero Beach, the major city had hundreds of people along the sidewalk witnessing the parade of cars. They knew that Fito was in one of the limousines and that the caravan was going to Valero Beach where Fito kept a large cruise ship. Tourists in Valero Beach were unaware of the significance of the noisy bands and at the same time, the empty main street of Valero Beach. Valero Beach was partially evacuated to prevent anyone from getting close to the caravan.

Close to mid-day, the caravan arrived at the dockside in the west side of Valero Beach.

The traditional annual parade took place at the "Plaza of the Republic." Fito, Ricardo, and their close supporters watched the military troops and worker's union members marching and displaying banners and signs, which read "Patria o Muerte"—country or death; "Venceremos"—we'll win; "Abajo el Imperialismo Yankee"—down with the Yankee Imperialists.

All this orchestrated propaganda was captured by the cameramen of local and international TV stations. However, the thousands who march on such a day were obligated by the union leaders to do so; if a worker refused, he could lose his job or be put in prison. The great majority of the people didn't agree with Fito's government. Nevertheless, they had no choice.

After three hours of the parade, Fito came to the microphone. He delivered another lengthy, meaningless speech. He talked about the hard times the country was enduring. He blamed the scarcity of goods once again on the merciless blockade imposed by the Americans. He described the recent killing of Isla Grande servicemen by the so-called "gusanos" who later escaped to the United States, and were encouraged by the wealthy, unpatriotic, right-wing Isla Grande exiles. He accused the United States of being an accomplice to these murders. Orchestrated applause and shouting by the crowd provided a colorful ambience. The monotonous repetition of the word FITO . . . . mesmerized the audience. It was a psychological method to distract the people and suppress momentarily their feelings of hunger and despair.

After his speech, Fito got into his Mercedes. His brother and several of his loyal private guards joined him. They drove to Valero Beach which is east of the capital of Isla Grande, a little over two hours away, escorted by dozens of private servicemen and loyal militia. This was another show of strength and power.

Fito and Ricardo spoke to each other. Ricardo said to Fito, "This is a real celebration that we will always remember. The revolution has persisted despite the numerous difficulties such as the lack of financial support from friendly countries to our revolution. We still have a large unemployment and rationing of food and other goods persists. I know we are hated outside and inside Isla Grande."

Fito replied, "Every attempt to topple our revolution has been unsuccessful. We have survived many crises and cannot expect things to get better until the blockade is lifted. We will have access to the international monetary fund. We will get loans that will help some of the rebuilding of our country, and, particularly, be able to feed Isla Grande citizens. All of us will be richer.

I can only think that the celebration of this 28th of July is a signal to the world of our strength and endurance." Minutes later he fell asleep for the rest of the trip.

CHAPTER 20

VALERO BEACH PARTY

At about 3 p.m. they arrived in Valero Beach, which is one of the most beautiful beaches in the world. On July 24, Ricardo had received a telegram from Hassan, who was in Mexico on his way to Miami, excusing himself for not attending the festivities. On the afternoon of July 28, Hassan left Miami for the Bahamas. He joined Eva, who flew first to Mexico, and then to Nassau, Bahamas. Hassan was following Alex's instructions.

The caravan reached Valero Beach and drove to the main dock where they boarded the Presidential Yacht for another party on the high seas. Ricardo informed Fito that shortly he would be surprised with an unforgettable gift and a unique experience. Fito didn't suspect for a moment what was awaiting him. A parade of government vessels and two Air Force helicopters accompanied the Presidential Yacht and cruised off the coast of Valero Beach. There was laughter, music and bikini-clad young women on board the Presidential Yacht.

Fito was an avid fisherman. He used to spear fish on many coral reefs that are abundant off the coast of Isla Grande. He and military personnel were the only ones allowed to fish. Any Isla Grande citizen who was caught fishing without a fishing permit was put in jail.

The people in Isla Grande profoundly resented the prohibition of fishing, although many, in the evening, did so to provide food for their starving family.

People who lived around Valero Beach and those who came from other cities to enjoy this fabulous resort, resented not only the fishing prohibition but the use of the beach facilities. One of the hotels was quite old. Fito had stayed at that hotel on his way to the capital and slept the night before his arrival at the capital to celebrate his revolution. There was a label on the door of the room saying that "Fito Slept Here."

The other hotels of Valero Beach were built in the last decade and most were owned by a private chain of hotels from Spain. The cost of the rooms and of the food was very reasonable. Valero Beach was crowded all months of the year, but particularly in winter between December and March. The airport, close to Valero Beach, allowed aircraft to land from the United States, Canada, Central and South America, and Europe. Most of the tourists were Canadians and Europeans.

Every hotel offered entertainment which sometimes was just a trio of singers and one or two dancers.

The visitors to Valero Beach were unaware of the extreme poverty of the island. They were exposed to small markets where handcrafted goods were sold for very little money.

As the economy of the island was based primarily, not on the export of goods, but on tourism, the government made it quite clear to the employees of the hotel that they had to cultivate and be as kind as possible to the tourists. At night there were buses taking the employees back to nearby cities. They were not allowed to stay at the beach, where only essential personnel were allowed after 6 p.m.

CHAPTER 21

THE DEMONSTRATION OF BLACKSHARK'S
SPECIAL FEATURES

Fito was informed that on the radio station, a familiar voice was heard on the speaker. Although Fito was partially drunk, he could recognize the voice of Ivan. He heard, "Fito, Fito, Ivan calling!"

"Boss; glorious 28th of July!" Ivan said. I'm bringing you a present that will halt the exodus of the so-called "gusanos." I'll demonstrate the unique features of this toy. Watch."

Fito looked through binoculars.

The awesome looking black vessel was seen about five miles away. Ivan, with Ricardo, had planned the show before his trip to Miami.

A small boat similar to **Cucaracha** was launched from one of Fito's patrol boats. Several cans with gasoline were placed in the little boat. Fito and his friends observed with binoculars what then happened.

Quico aimed the 30 mm cannon on board Blackshark at the small boat. When it appeared dead center on the TV screen, and while traveling at 40 mph and jumping over the waves, he fired. Accurately, the missile hit the small boat, blowing it into uncountable pieces. The spectacular explosion was followed by the enthusiastic applause of the Islanders who were observing the show from the government ship.

Immediately thereafter, a small blimp was released from the same patrol vessel which launched the small boat. A basket under the balloon aircraft was also filled with several cans of fuel. The balloon rose into the sky and when it was almost halfway between Blackshark and the Presidential Yacht, Miguel aimed the .50 cal. machine gun and blew up the balloon. Another explosion, this time in the sky, created sinister fireworks which amused and impressed the surprised Fito and his jackals.

Ivan then addressed his boss saying, "Fito, what you have seen is just a small example of what Blackshark can do. At night, she uses infrared lights, lasers, and sensors, to identify and destroy any floating or airborne target. At this distance of about three miles from your lovely yacht, I can spot the derriere of the beautiful brunette wearing a golden tanga, and standing by you." There was another big laugh from the dictator's men.

Tourists watched from a distance smoke in the air and explosions that looked like fireworks. "How could there be fireworks if it was daytime!" said one of the tourists.

No one was allowed to walk on the beach towards the western part of Valero Beach.

People at the dock wondered what had happened since on previous occasions they had never heard sounds of machine guns or noises which appeared not to be a threat to Fito's vessel. Those who lived in Valero Beach and worked primarily with tourism were surprised to see so much activity, although they realized that July 28 was a day of celebration.

CHAPTER 22

THE RECOVERY OF BLACKSHARK
AND THE END OF A DICTATORSHIP

While watching the frenzy of Ivan and his assistants, Simon, Tony, and Everett were able to untie themselves. They jumped the surprised Ivan, Quico and Miguel. They struggled and for a moment, Blackshark zig-zagged out of control. Ivan, Quico, and Miguel were overpowered and immobilized. Fito watched from his boat and shouted to Ivan, "Are you drunk again? What's going on?" Tony, Simon's brother spoke on the radio, imitating Ivan's voice. "Boss, don't worry, I became distracted for a few moments watching your spectacular female companions." There was another laugh on Fito's boat.

Simon and his crew had regained control of Blackshark and its weapons. The occupants of the Isla Grande boats didn't realize that Blackshark had a new crew. Ivan, Quico, and Miguel were now the prisoners of the good guys.

Simon, at the helm of the boat, made a 90 degree turn and aimed the bow and its cannon at Fito's yacht. Tony looked into the attack console video screen and when the dictator's yacht was in the center of the screen, he activated the cannon. A few seconds later a loud blast was heard. Fito's yacht was blown up in myriads of pieces. There was an uncontrollable fire in the Presidential Yacht. The blast and the fire left no survivors. Bodies and pieces of servicemen were spotted floating on the water. One of these was Fito. The patrol boats and the helicopters watched astonished at the macabre scene. As they were caught by surprise, they didn't know what to do. No one aboard the Presidential Yacht was still alive. An officer from one of the patrol boats shouted into his radiomicrophone, "Let's kill these bastards!"

The waters around the Presidential Yacht were covered by an oil spill. Blazing fires surrounded the Yacht. There was a great deal of confusion. The only aggressor appeared to come from the black vessel, which was originally thought to represent an ally of Fito's regime.

Because Blackshark was originally coursing towards the Presidential Yacht and suddenly turned away from the yacht, following a northwest direction, it became obvious that the occupants of Blackshark were running away. This triggered an immediate reaction of the patrol boats, helicopters, and aircraft, who decided to destroy Blackshark.

This event undoubtedly was a great surprise. Strict measures for the protection of Fito and the hierarchy of the revolution were followed. Starting with the caravan trajectory to the boarding of Fito's yacht and the cruising paralleling Valero Beach, it was a protected journey from land, water, and air. In the air there were helicopters. The only unusual occurrence was the presence of a black vessel which was spotted by the helicopters. Patrol boats preceded the presidential yacht and surrounded it. Occasionally Fito enjoyed skin-diving and a reserved area around the ship was heavily guarded.

At this time Fito was enjoying the party with his brother and acquaintances.

CHAPTER 23

THE PURSUIT OF BLACKSHARK

Immediately upon succeeding in the destruction of the Presidential Yacht, the crew of Blackshark threw Ivan and his two companions overboard. They were left floating with life jackets. Ivan protested and cursed.

"Enjoy what so many thousands of our compatriots have felt when left adrift in this vast ocean. If you ever return to Isla Grande, you will be considered a traitor," Simon said to Ivan. "Someone will take care of you and your companions. Goodbye."

Little did Simon know that his encounter with the Islanders wouldn't be over.

Blackshark made a sharp 180 degree turn and headed toward Key West. The Isla Grande patrol vessels started the chase of Blackshark. Two fast speedboats ran in the direction of Blackshark and cruised at a slightly higher speed. Helicopters flew toward Blackshark.

Simon and his two companions put on their helmets and their protective suits. Torpedoes were launched from the Isla Grande Coast Guard vessels and headed toward Blackshark. The magnetic diversion device was engaged. As the torpedoes approached Blackshark, the magnetic fields diverted the course of the torpedoes.

The two Isla Grande high-speed patrol boats fired at Blackshark. Many of the bullets missed because the machine guns moved up and down following the motion of the boats. They didn't have the stabilization mechanism of the weapons installed on Blackshark. Some of the bullets hit Blackshark but the reinforced hull prevented the bullets from causing any significant damage.

Two helicopters stalked Blackshark. Simon then activated the smoke mechanism. A cloud formed over Blackshark and several clouds appeared in front and to the sides. This confused the helicopter pilots who could no longer observe the vessel under them. They hopelessly and aimlessly fired their machine guns. The helmets and protective suits protected the crew. The reinforced deck prevented damage to the vessel.

Everett activated his machine gun and aimed it at the two helicopters. He successfully blew them up. He then turned the machine guns towards the speedboats and they were also successfully destroyed. They all laughed and congratulated each other. The speed of Blackshark exceeded that of the remaining Isla Grande patrol boats and after a few minutes, Blackshark was left alone, cruising at high speed towards Key West.

As they had fueled in Key West, the vessel was able to make the trip back to the United States without the need for additional fueling.

All the weaponry on board the vessel and the necessary protection, such as the reinforced hull, the special garments and the smoke-producing devices had saved their lives.

Prior to arriving in Key West, the cannon and the machine gun were covered. Bullets were dumped into the ocean and the helmets and protective garments were properly stored.

Everett asked Simon and Peter, "Should we jump in the ocean and refresh before we go on television?" Simon replied, "I don't believe we have to waste any more time. I am concerned about a small vessel which was seen on the way to Valero Beach. I wonder if we can spot some rafters."

Peter used binoculars and reported, "I see no one nor a vessel for as far as I can observe the ocean."

It was a beautiful afternoon. At this time of the year it gets dark after 8 p.m. Blackshark was making excellent time and soon they were successful in reaching Key West.

CHAPTER 24

RESCUING CUCARACHA'S OCCUPANTS

Lidia and Mario were adrift for hours. Both wore life jackets and Mario kept holding on to one of the oars of the small boat. Mario suddenly looked into the sky and said to Lidia, "I hear the noise of an airplane."

"Why don't we place my necklace with the charm on the end of the oar?" Lidia responded. "The reflections of the sun on the faceted surfaces of the sphere may act as a beacon. We may be detected by the aircraft." They quickly attached the necklace to the paddle of the oar and Mario waved it, holding the other end. He waved the oar in a circular manner. The small faceted sphere of Lidia's charm reflected the sunlight.

The Rescue Brothers is a not-for-profit organization of volunteer Cuban pilots which have been cruising the Florida Straits for years. They do not have the authority of providing direct services to rafters except identifying where they are and relating the information to the Coast Guard. Thanks to their efforts, hundreds of rafters have been discovered and eventually saved from drowning or their killing by sharks. Three of these small airplanes were gunned down by Russian-built MIGS. The pilots who were killed are martyrs and their memories will be kept alive for years to come.

In the last few years, the mission of the Rescue Brothers has been terminated. The only protests that have taken place are fleets of unarmed vessels that have departed from Key West and have stopped in international waters, releasing balloons and firecrackers so the people in the island can see them from a distance. These peaceful demonstrations have been aimed to maintain the spirit of the islanders and remind them that there are hundreds of exiles that care for them.

An observer for Rescue Brothers, the airplane which was flying close by, was scanning the surface of the ocean with binoculars. He suddenly detected a bright intermittent, weak flashing light from a tiny spot on the surface of the ocean. "Fly lower," he shouted to the pilot. "I believe I see something down there, not a boat, but there is a very unusual reflection coming from the surface of the ocean."

At this time of day, the sun rays shone at an angle and oblique rays reflected from the surfaces of the charm. The crew of the aircraft spotted the two who were floating next to each other. Rescue Brothers immediately notified the U.S. Coast Guard that two people were floating on the ocean with no vessels in sight. They flew in tight circles above the survivors. They shouted, saying, "Be patient, you will be rescued soon." The fin of a large shark could be seen close by. A fishing boat nearby heard the conversation between the airplane and the Coast Guard and arrived to the place where Lidia and Mario were floating in the water, rescued them and brought them close to Marathon Key. The owner of the fishing boat was also from Isla Grande and had escaped several years before. He knew that if the Coast Guard would have rescued Lidia and Mario, they would have been returned to Isla Grande.

This is how Lidia and Mario set foot on U.S. soil. The fishing boat crew never revealed what they had done (which was illegal). The Coast Guard never found Lidia and Mario.

The object of the rafters is to touch land. They will not be returned to the island if they reach land in the United States. If the Coast Guard rescues a rafter, by law they must be returned to Isla Granda.

The frustrations of rafters who adventure and escape from the island and risk their lives to be returned to the island is a terrible experience. When back in the island, the government either puts them in jail or deprives them of the basic means of making a living.

At one time there was a large exodus from Isla Grande to the United States. Thousands arrived in Florida. Many were prisoners and also patients from mental health hospitals. In addition, there were many spies of the regime. This gave the Isla Grande government the opportunity of getting rid of thousands of people who they considered a burden. It also provided them with the opportunity of introducing to American soil, spies for the regime.

If a vessel picks up a rafter and doesn't report it to the Coast Guard, they are at risk of going to jail and losing their vessel. Lidia and Mario were very fortunate to have been picked up by a fishing boat with a sympathetic crew.

CHAPTER 25

THE ARRIVAL OF BLACKSHARK IN KEY WEST

Blackshark, in less than two hours, arrived in Key West. It was a beautiful bright afternoon with a lovely sunset. People crowded the sundecks of hotels located in the southern tip of Key West. It was common for people to watch the sunset there every evening—it is magnificent. Many stared at the incoming black vessel with its awesome appearance. They waved at the three crew members of Blackshark. Blackshark slowly moved toward the fueling station. The same U.S. Coast Guard vessel which had greeted Blackshark passed by and the Captain asked, "How was the testing?"

Simon answered with a big smile, "We had a great time. Everything went perfectly, as anticipated, and we are ready to go back home."

Simon, Tony and Everett approached the fuel station where they had been earlier that morning. The fuel station was deserted; they had already closed. Tony and Everett located and then convinced the owner to supply them with fuel because they had to return to Miami that same evening. While they were refueling Blackshark, Simon went to a pay phone in the Marina and called Alex. He informed him what had happened and said, "Alex, the mission has been successfully accomplished. We will celebrate tomorrow in Miami."

"Did anyone get hurt?" Alex asked.

"We had a minimal altercation on board Blackshark," Simon replied, "but were able to get rid of the 'big, as well as the small fishes.' I am calling you from a fueling dock in Key West and we are heading back to Miami as soon as we fuel the boat. We hope to arrive late tonight and I will touch base with you tomorrow."

"Your gift will be in your hands tomorrow," Alex said. "God has been on our side. You will become a hero, if you so wish."

"I want no publicity. My plans are to go back to my country and help in rebuilding Isla Grande."

"God bless you all. Have a safe trip back."

Alex quickly contacted all the members of the Council of International Affairs who financed the Omega Project. He was very brief on the phone. He suggested having a meeting at mid-day the next day and they all accepted.

CHAPTER 26

THE ALCANIAN AMBASSADOR IN THE BAHAMAS

On the beautiful beach of Paradise Island in Nassau, Bahamas, Hassan had been basking in the sun on the afternoon of July 28. He held in his hand a tropical drink.

Next to him was Eva, his lovely blonde companion. His cellular phone rang and he promptly answered. He heard the familiar voice of Alex, who said, "Hassan, I have good news for you. The mission has been successfully accomplished. As promised, you will receive your gift tomorrow. Good luck."

Hassan looked at Eva and said, "Darling, we have a lot to celebrate. Cheers!" They touched their two glasses, took a sip, gave each other a kiss, and turned their faces toward the beautiful sunset.

Hassan, later made the following comment, without explaining to Eva the details of the Omega Project.

"It gives us a wonderful feeling when we do a good deed and get paid for it!!! Our mission in life is to love, be happy, make others happy, and make positive contributions to make the world a better place to live. A friend told me once that—It doesn't matter what we do in life; what matters is what we leave behind . . .

What we have done for ourselves alone, dies with us; what we have done for others and the world, is immortal.

I don't consider myself as being a good person. However, I have made possible a change which will make many, many people happy. We deserve what is coming to us" (he was thinking of the check he would receive the following day).

Eva replied: "Hassan you are a good man. For whatever you have done, you deserve all the wonderful things that will be come to you." . . . Could we get married in the Bahamas?"

Hassan was surprised; he said, "Yes, indeed! You are the best thing that ever happened to me." "To us." They made another toast with champagne.

Nassau is the capital of the Bahamas. It has been famous for gambling and for offering all types of water attractions. There is fishing (conventional and spear-fishing), cruising to other islands, and simply cruising at sunset. It has the most expensive hotel ever built on a Caribbean island.

The Bahamas have been a haven for wealthy people who have used the Bahamian banks as a shelter to avoid taxes.

Hassan and Eva knew it was a safe place and certainly a most enjoyable one to live the lifestyle of a perennial tourist.

CHAPTER 27

CELEBRATION BY AN EXILE GROUP

In the morning of July 29 and on a beach in the Florida Keys, Lidia and Mario hugged and kissed each other, and then knelt and kissed the ground. Relatives and friends had been contacted by the vessel that rescued them from the ocean. They surrounded and embraced them. They all held hands, closed their eyes, and prayed to Heaven, expressing gratitude to God for the privilege of being alive, safe, and well.

Lidia and Mario turned their eyes toward the ocean and Mario said haltingly, "For the thousands of my fellow men who cannot share these moments, my deepest respect. We hope we meet some day in Heaven. May your efforts be remembered as an example of courage, dignity, tenacity, and, unfortunately, fruitless expectation."

At a distance, a small vessel floated on the ocean. It was **Cucaracha**!

It is estimated that only one (or less) of every eight people who tried to reach the United States in a primitive vessel, made it. The majority drowned. Many were picked up by the US Coast Guard and returned to their homeland.

Children have been sent to the United States leaving their parents behind. The United States' generosity has been shown in many ways for many years. The breaking up of families, the continued suffering and the struggling to survive in Isla Grande, the imprisonment of hundreds of people whose only reason for being put in jail was because they peacefully protested against a long-lasting dictatorship, are among the many reasons that organizations like the United Nations should act swiftly when similar circumstances oppress a nation.

When rafters arrive to the Florida Keys they are taken to a temporary detention camp. They go through a thorough medical check-up and have to complete a considerable number of documents. Most of the rafters have relatives or friends which is the first step towards settling in Florida or in other states of the Union. Those who do not have family or friends are given the opportunity of temporarily getting food stamps and housing. Based on their skills, every effort is made to find them a job.

Immigrants who reach the United States create a very serious social problem. They compete for jobs with legalized and American-born citizens. There have been numerous altercations among immigrants and Americans because the former have taken jobs away from American citizens.

Recent governments have made extensive efforts to send back to their countries those who have illegally settled in the United States. However, immigrants from certain countries, particularly Isla Grande, are given the right to settle due to the fact that it was a humanitarian effort to accept people who risk their lives to come to a free country.

CHAPTER 28

SIMON'S STRATEGY

Following the refueling of Blackshark, and the telephone conversation with Alex, Simon returned to the fueling dock. He boarded Blackshark and he, Tony, and Everett headed back to Miami. Cruising at low speed around the southern tip of Key West, Simon addressed his friends.

"What happened today will have international repercussions. I suggest that we carefully answer the numerous questions they'll ask us. Our boss in Miami, the press, and government authorities will ask the same things. We must tell them the truth."

Then he paused. "Almost all the truth. The truth is that Blackshark was seized by Ivan and his two assistants who tied us up and executed specific plans which led to the trip to Isla Grande. We must say that Ivan and his friends were double agents; that they seized the boat with the objective of blowing up the Presidential Yacht. We'll say that we assume they must have been paid a considerable amount of money to do so."

"After they succeeded in their mission, they untied us, jumped into the ocean, swam towards a nearby Isla Grande patrol boat, and told us to head back to Miami, that they didn't need the boat anymore. We turned the boat around and had to fight Isla Grande patrol boats and helicopters trying to destroy us. They were under the assumption that we were the ones who caused the catastrophe. Let the world put the blame on Ivan and his friends. We simply were lucky to save our lives and to get back to the United States. If we told the whole truth, we would be accused of premeditation and of carrying out an act of war. We would be put in prison. This should be all that we say."

"Not only are you my older brother, but continue being the smartest," Tony replied.

Everett then spoke up. "We are all brothers and must stick together. If we were to reveal the truth, not only would we lose our jobs at the Mag Company, but would have to pay the damages. I have a family to support and I want to keep it low key. I agree with Simon, and what you have just suggested is the policy that we will follow."

Simon, Tony, and Everett arrived in Miami a little after midnight on July 29. When they turned on the radio, confusing news was being aired. On some stations, they said that something strange had happened in Isla Grande. The newscasters said that the rumor was that Fito became suddenly ill and was hospitalized. A report from CNN indicated that a strange explosion had occurred off the coast of Valero Beach. Tourists and Islanders were all alarmed when they observed helicopters and patrol boats heading toward the United States. Are they planning an invasion of the Florida Keys? What caused the explosion?

Simon looked at Tony and Everett and smiled. "We really know what happened. Soon they will come to realize that Isla Grande finally is free and that a new golden age waits for the Islanders in Isla Grande and those who are exiled in so many countries around the world."

Everett suggested, "Let's have a drink and start celebrating."

Simon replied, "Everett, we need to be as sober as possible. We are going to be bombarded by questions asked by many reporters. We have to rehearse what we are going to say so there is consistency. We should all be together but it is conceivable that some of us may be cornered by newspapermen and women to further clarify what has happened. They discussed in detail the answers that they planned to give when briefed at the Mag Company.

CHAPTER 29

BRIEFING AT THE MAG COMPANY ON JULY 29

Early on the morning of July 29, the owner and personnel of the Mag Company came to the dock and were amazed to see Blackshark. It looked like a disabled vessel. The hull was dented, undoubtedly by bullet marks, as was the deck. The rest of the boat seemed to be in good order.

Simon, Everett, and Tony arrived around a quarter to eight in the evening. They appeared tired, but at the same time they had an expression of happiness. They looked like children who had performed the forbidden and were glad that they did it. The owner of the Mag Company asked Simon, "What happened?"

"Thank God we are alive and Blackshark is back at home. Yesterday, early in the morning, your client, Ivan, boarded the boat with us and we made it quickly and safely to Key West. In Key West we fueled the boat and planned to return to Miami. Ivan's two friends boarded the boat asking for a free ride to Miami."

"As soon as we got into Hawk Channel, Ivan and his two friends pulled guns and seized the boat. We were tied, and became witness to an amazing experience. Ivan took control of the boat and headed towards Isla Grande. About two and a half hours later we could see at a distance the coast of the Matilda Province and the beautiful, long sandy beach of Valero. We could also see one large vessel and numerous Isla Grande patrol boats. There were two helicopters flying close to what appeared to be the Presidential Yacht. Ivan directed Blackshark towards the Presidential Yacht and Quico, one of his assistants, fired the cannon. He was right on target and we could see from a distance of about three and a half miles, the blowing up of the Presidential Yacht."

"Blackshark continued towards the Presidential Yacht and made a sudden 90 degree turn when it was about 500 yards from an Isla Grande patrol boat. Ivan untied us and he, Quico, and Miguel jumped into the water, saying, "Take it back, our mission has been accomplished. They swam toward a patrol boat.""

"We took control of Blackshark and turned around and headed towards the Florida Keys. To our surprise, two Isla Grande speedboats started chasing us. The Isla Grande patrol boats were slower than Blackshark but they fired their machine guns at us. They wanted to destroy us!"

"Two helicopters flew over Blackshark and also started firing from above. We were able to protect ourselves and the vessel. Everett shot down the two helicopters and also blew up the two speedboats. The Isla Grande patrol boats were slower than Blackshark and they were unable to reach us."

"When we were out of reach, we headed straight to Key West. We felt it was best to bring what happened to your attention before we make a public statement."

The owner of Mag Company said, "Thank God, the three of you are safe. We are going to have to call our Coast Guard and hope that they don't penalize you and the Company for not reporting this event immediately upon your return to Key West. We will also initiate immediate legal action against Mr. Hassan."

John, the foreman of the Mag Company, commented, "Last night and today we have been listening to the radio and watching television news. Apparently something serious happened in Isla Grande. They don't know the truth. Many rumors express the concern of the Islanders. The Isla Grande exiles seem to be in an uproar. Some believe this is another false alarm and that nothing has happened to Fito, the Isla Grande dictator. Others think that perhaps there has been an attempt to kill Fito and hope it was successful."

Simon, Tony, and Everett moved indoors and then the owner of the Mag Company made a call to the Coast Guard.

The Coast Guard representatives went to the Mag Company and asked Simon, Tony, and Everett to relate what had happened. They repeated their statement. The three were asked why they didn't file a report of their mishap when they arrived in Key West.

"We were shaken up and just wanted to get back to Miami," Simon said. Simon, Tony and Everett were reprimanded by the Coast Guard authorities.

The following day, on the front pages of U.S. newspapers and flashed across TV screens were pictures of Simon, Tony, and Everett and the bullet-pockmarked Blackshark. The caption read, "Could this vessel have played a part in the end of the dictatorship in Isla Grande?"

Simon, Tony, and Everett were heroes, although they denied blowing up the Presidential Yacht.

CHAPTER 30

URGENT MEETING OF THE COUNCIL OF ISLA GRANDE AFFAIRS ON THE MORNING OF JULY 29

Alex called a meeting of the Council of Isla Grande Affairs. All except Mario attended the meeting which was held at 10:00 a.m. at the same private club where Alex presented the Omega Project. Alex said, addressing the group, "Our mission has been successful. The Isla Grande dictator has been blown to kingdom come. We believe that his brother and their closest friends also were eliminated."

"Innocent lives have been spared, thanks to the detailed planning, your huge support, and the successful implementation of the Omega Project. We should all be elated, yet it is essential that none of us reveal the secret of the Omega Project. Not only could we end up in jail for promoting the accident from the United States, but we may be all called to pay with imprisonment and with dollars for inflicted damage."

"At this time we do not know what is happening in Isla Grande. We suspect that a dramatic change will occur. I have called Mario on the phone and have informed him about our meeting today. He understands that we must remain silent."

"I would now like to propose a toast and make a suggestion." A bottle of champagne was opened.

"Isn't it too early to drink champagne?" Fernando asked.

"This is a unique, historical moment and I urge that not only do we drink to the ending of four decades of dictatorship, but that we all pray in silence in memory of those who lost their lives and in gratitude for the success of the Omega Project," Leslie replied.

They all knelt. Isaac remained standing, but with his head bowed and his eyes closed. They all prayed to God. "Thank you, God, for allowing us to participate in this historical event," Leslie said. "We made a pledge to work, use any available resource, to provoke a change and the change has occurred. We now pledge to continue helping, not only Isla Grande, but the country which has made it possible for us to become wealthy and to use part of our wealth in the meaningful cause, the United States of America. We all are citizens of two countries and it is like having two children. We love them both." They stood up, opened the champagne, poured the champagne into glasses, and made a toast. "Salud!" "Cheers!"

Alex then made another transcendental proposal. "Our job is not over. We must pray to God that the change in Isla Grande will bring back democracy and that the bloodshed that we all expect will not occur. Many Islanders who supported Fito deserve punishment. They will be punished."

"I suggest that as senior life members of the Council of Isla Grande Affairs, we start a fund that will help in the restoration of Isla Grande. What I propose is that we bring into the club individuals who will donate monies which will be used for humanitarian missions."

"Carlos, you are a lawyer. You can create a nonprofit organization. What I suggest is that the proceeds of this fund be utilized to support one or several projects to be approved by the Executive Board of the Council of Isla Grande Affairs. In other words, if we raise several million dollars, the interest of that money will be used exclusively to promote health, education, start new businesses, grant scholarships, etc. The projects will be suggested by all the membership and the Executive Board will prioritize them and then submit to them a vote of all the members of the Council of Isla Grande Affairs. The capital should always remain in the United States. Only the interest of this fund will be utilized for specific projects, such as those I have outlined."

"Well, this seems like a very feasible plan," Carlos said. "As you know, many of us will do business in Isla Grande. Some of the proceeds of those businesses will be utilized in Isla Grande and we can also use some of the profits to beef up the fund of the Council of Isla Grande Affairs."

Alex turned to Felipe. "We know that you are ready to export medications. There are several organizations that will have to be quickly mobilized. The immediate needs in Isla Grande are food and medical supplies. The latter is in your domain. This is the moment that you have been waiting for."

He turned to Aurelio saying, "You have food markets and contacts with food distributors. You and Felipe are going to be the most active members of this group. We can all help you by giving you monies to buy more food staples. I wish you luck in establishing markets in Isla Grande."

"I am ready," Aurelio said, "and I will proceed through the appropriate authorities to export food immediately."

"Initially, the vehicle that the American Jewish Federation has utilized seems to me to be the most practical way of distributing food supplies and medications in the island," Isaac mentioned. "We have used the synagogues, and suggest that churches and other nonprofit organizations be utilized as intermediaries between us, the United States, and the Isla Grande government. First, we must ensure what kind of government will replace Fito."

Jose spoke up. "It is a shame that we did not raise more than three million dollars. These monies have been already utilized. I will keep the account open and let it be utilized by the Council of Isla Grande Affairs to generate the funds mentioned by Alex."

All the other members of the Council made brief speeches. They committed to meet regularly the last Thursday evening of every month. Ramon volunteered to put together a newsletter which would be circulated monthly among the members of the Council of Isla Grande Affairs.

Armando mentioned that he would contact other organized groups in exile and inform them about the project of creating a fund.

Armando said, "We should pool resources. Everyone will have a voice in the Council of Isla Grande Affairs. The Executive Committee would only become a vehicle to implement the various projects." The meeting was over around 11:30 a.m.

CHAPTER 31

CHAOS AND JUBILEE IN ISLA GRANDE

The headlines in the main Isla Grande newspaper the morning of July 29 read:

A SINISTER EXPLOSION OFF THE COAST OF VALERO BEACH

At this time we do not know the whereabouts of Fito, his brother, and the executives of our government. We suspect there has been an attack by air and water from the United States and that they have attacked our country once again.

On the streets of the capital of Isla Grande and throughout the island, people shouted, "Down with Fito, the time has come to start a new life!"

There were numerous fights on the streets between the Islanders and the military, particularly the members of the Brigades of Rapid Action. In the larger cities, sirens were heard. Some were police cars, others were fire trucks trying to stop the fires that were set in numerous buildings. Some were government buildings. Police cars were turned over and set on fire.

Tanks patrolled the periphery of the Colonia camp and were positioned at key posts in the city. The main roads that led in and out of the cities, such as the capital of Isla Grande, were blocked by tanks and police cars. It seemed as if all the military forces were ordered into the streets to stop the chaos and revolt of the Isla Grande citizens.

At Colonia, General Cortinas and General Rodriguez, two low-key, highly respected professionals in their late 60's, met in Ricardo's office.

"We don't know the whereabouts of Ricardo and Fito," Cortinas said. "We are senior members of the military force and I suggest we take charge of the army. We should stop this massacre of people. It seems that the time has come when a change, expected by everyone, takes place."

They immediately called for a meeting of the armed forces and General Rodriguez spoke. He said that they were jointly taking charge of the armed forces and that they were ordering that the killing of innocent people cease immediately. General Cortinas mentioned that he had been contacted by telephone from Valero Beach and that no one knew the whereabouts of Fito and Ricardo; the Presidential Yacht had been hit and destroyed.

"There is a strong possibility that Fito and all the other occupants have been killed," said General Cortinas. The soldiers who were listening looked at each other. Some threw their hats in the air and said, "Finally, we are free of tyranny!"

General Rodriguez said that he was calling the radio stations to broadcast that he and General Cortinas were establishing a temporary military government and that they were requesting the citizens to remain calm and stop the riots. After the speech in Colonia, they boarded a military vehicle and headed toward the Government Palace. At the Government Palace, the guards offered no resistance. They entered the Palace and went directly to Fito's office where they contacted the radio stations, the newspapers, and produced an official statement indicating that, because of the disappearance of Fito, Ricardo, and Fito's personal guard, a new temporary government was being established. It would be directed by General Cortinas and General Rodriguez. These two generals were highly respected by both the old and the young officers of Fito's military force.

On the streets, fights continued, not only between the members of the armed forces and the Isla Grande citizens, but among the soldiers. Some, particularly those who belonged to the Brigade of Rapid Action, killed and injured unarmed Islanders. Many soldiers who did not care to hurt their own brothers, decided to fight pro-Fito's men.

Loudspeakers were heard and radio announcements were made indicating a change in the Isla Grande government and establishment of a new military regime under Generals Cortinas and Rodriguez. The fights continued for more than 24 hours. Entire cities were left in shambles. The Islanders became exhausted. Some were drunk and continued to fight. All the businesses stopped. The country became paralyzed. It seemed that this was the longest day in the history of Isla Grande. Virtually no one slept; some because of exhaustion, others because of happiness, fear or uncertainty.

CHAPTER 32

MEETING AT THE PENTAGON
AND THE STATE DEPARTMENT

General Robinson from the Pentagon, the Secretary of Defense, and the hierarchy of the State Department met urgently on July 29 in Washington. General Robinson said that he had given instructions to the American ships in the military base in Isla Grande and throughout the Caribbean to proceed towards Isla Grande yet remain in international waters close to the capital of Isla Grande and the major cities.

General Robinson reported that reliable sources from Miami had related an episode that involved a special patrol boat built by the Mag Company. He said that apparently Arab terrorists took over the control of this boat. They succeeded in their mission to destroy the Presidential Yacht which had on board Fito, Ricardo, and his closest followers. No one knew the whereabouts of these Arab terrorists.

General Robinson continued, "We must not make rapid, drastic decisions until we have all the facts. At this time, the briefing of the three American crew members who were in the boat called Blackshark has been concluded. This is the only reliable source we have to establish what truly happened to Fito and his men."

Mr. Warren, of the State Department, mentioned, "We have reports from Isla Grande that a temporary government has been established. General Cortinas and General Rodriguez have contacted the White House and the Pentagon and have requested help, not only from the Isla Grande government, but also from the Isla Grande exiles.

We have given instructions that no one is to go into or leave Isla Grande until all facts are known and we decide the direction to be followed. Our Coast Guard patrolling the Florida peninsula will abort vessels attempting a trip to Isla Grande. We have requested Central and South American countries, Canada, and European countries to stop their flights into Isla Grande. We are going to send an immediate delegation from the State Department to the capital of Isla Grande to speak to Generals Cortinas and Rodriguez. We do not want to give the impression that the United States is going to invade the island."

General Robinson and Mr. Warren drove immediately to the White House.

The President had returned from his vacation retreat to the White House. Members of the press were waiting for a formal declaration. The President met first privately with General Robinson and Mr. Warren. He was informed of all the recent developments.

At noon on July 29, the President called a press conference. He stated that there was reason to believe that dictator Fito, his brother, and key supporters had lost their lives in an accident. Isla Grande was under a new temporary government.

He mentioned that the White House had already made plans to appoint ten Islanders in exile to become intermediaries between the temporary government of Isla Grande and the United States. Their mission was for them to be recipients of humanitarian help that will come from the United States, and, also, from the International Red Cross.

"Will the United States re-establish diplomatic relations with Isla Grande?"

"If we see that the democratization of Isla Grande is becoming a reality, the answer is yes," the President replied. "We will assist in every way possible in the restoration of democracy in Isla Grande."

"Mr. President, another question. Will the United States allow the Islanders to leave Isla Grande and migrate to the United States?"

"We have made provisions to accept only those who have relatives here and those who will come on a temporary basis. It will be no different than others who come with a tourist visa from another country. Our immigration policy, for the time being, will not be changed."

"What will happen in South Florida? Will all the Islanders leave for Isla Grande?"

"I have been informed that probably 10 to 15 percent of Islanders in exile will return to Isla Grande," the President replied. "On the other hand, I have been informed that a similar number of people may come to the United States, once again, on a temporary basis. I do not believe that in the near future there will be any negative financial impact on South Florida by the democratization of Isla Grande. We have been informed that Islanders and the ones who became naturalized American citizens are eager to establish new businesses there.

There remains a lot to be done. The whole island has been destroyed by four decades of dictatorship. It will take years, probably no less than five, to repair the damage and restore the island."

With those words, the President ended the press conference and retired.

CNN was transmitting from Valero Beach and from the capital of Isla Grande. The TV newscasters, based on reliable sources, reported that the Presidential Yacht had been destroyed on the afternoon of July 28 when Fito and Ricardo were on board. They mentioned there were no survivors from the large explosion. "There is a lot of speculation as to who caused the attack. All the facts indicate this was not an accident. A strange, mysterious, black vessel was seen in the vicinity of the Isla Grande boats before the explosion. What was initially thought to be a possible attack off the Isla Grande coast by Island exiles, turned out to be the chase of that black boat by Isla Grande patrol boats and helicopters."

"Soon after the big explosion, other smaller explosions were seen at a distance. Smoke was observed and we do not know at this time if the Isla Grande patrol boats succeeded in destroying the black boat, or whether Isla Grande patrol boats and helicopters have been destroyed. There is a lot of speculation as to what happened, but the only thing that we can say is that Fito, his brother, and close assistants have been killed."

CHAPTER 33

THE BEGINNING OF A NEW ERA

The leadership of Isla Grande exile groups called for an urgent meeting, moderated by Anthony, a highly respected Isla Grande economist who was not a politician and did not belong to any of the Isla Grande exile parties. He said that this was the golden opportunity for the exiles from Isla Grande to stop the bloodshed and help with the reconstruction of Isla Grande. He mentioned that the common goal of all the Isla Grande exile groups was to topple the government and that this already had occurred. The second common goal was to help in the democratization and rebuilding of Isla Grande. "Personal ambitions," he said, "should be set aside. We must meet with the ten individuals appointed by the State Department to help the temporary government in Isla Grande."

"Are the ten members of the Isla Grande exiles selected by the State Department members of our group?" George asked.

"We have been informed that they are a group of people who will act as intermediaries between the U.S. government and the Isla Grande government," Anthony replied. "At this point in time, they are not expected to become active in the new Isla Grande government. They will not be a policy-forming body. Some are members of Isla Grande exile organizations."

A member of the State Department arrived and soon addressed the group. "I have instructions from the President of the United States, the Pentagon, and the State Department, to proffer an official statement and make a specific request."

"The statement is that a new era in Isla Grande has begun. A military government is going to rule temporarily and prevent further bloodshed. They have requested that members of the Human Rights Committee and representatives of the Isla Grande exile groups that you represent join the delegation of ten individuals we have appointed. General Cortinas and General Rodriguez, with a group of Islanders, will form a temporary government. They will establish areas of responsibilities, assign individuals for specific tasks, and will establish priorities."

"It is our sincere hope that all the goods and help that will be delivered to Isla Grande will reach and satisfy the immediate needs of the population. There should be no waste and confusion, as unfortunately occurred with the humanitarian help we gave to the victims of the disaster of Hurricane Andrew. At that time, food and clothing became spoiled because of a poor system for distribution of these products."

"In Isla Grande, we have decided that the ten American naturalized Islanders selected by the State Department will be the ones to act as intermediaries between the U.S. and Isla Grande. We will deliver first only essential items: foods and medicines. There is a lot of work to be done and we hope that the exile groups will help through their delegations."

Anthony asked the American official, "Will we be able to go to Isla Grande and participate in the government?"

The American officer responded, "By all means, we all need each other. Our role is to simply ensure that there will never again be a dictatorship and that the transition takes place in an orderly fashion."

"We will soon restore air travel into and from the island and will allow vessels to leave Florida for Isla Grande. Under no circumstances will another massive exodus of Islanders from the island be allowed. Those who are detained in many American cities, those who have been living in the Bahamas, Central and South American countries, will be offered free transportation back to Isla Grande whenever they so wish."

"Please remain calm. We do not want the bloodshed to continue. Unless there is peace in Isla Grande, free access into the island will not be allowed."

He then left and the group continued talking among themselves. They came to realize that their prayers had been heard. On the evening of July 29, masses were held throughout many churches in the United States. Americans, and exiles from Isla Grande, as well as South Americans who were in sympathy with the Isla Grande exiles, joined in prayer.

The newspapers in the United States, television broadcasts, and all news media announced that the dictatorship of four decades had ended and that a new era for Isla Grande had begun.

CHAPTER 34

SIMON IN ISLA GRANDE

About two weeks after the episode of July 28, Simon informed the President of Mag Company that he and Tony were returning to Isla Grande to help in the restoration of democracy. They were requesting a leave of absence.

Simon and Tony boarded an airplane in Miami and landed in the capital of Isla Grande. The Isla Grande press and the foreign press knew they were coming and waited for their airplane to arrive. At the Airport, they were surrounded by reporters. Little did Simon and Tony suspect that a serious problem would occur.

Simon got on the microphone and spoke to the jubilant crowd, "Through the many centuries of man's existence, ruthless dictators have taken over governments, sometimes ruling for a considerable period of time. Man, by nature, is not interested in wars. By his instincts and his education, he knows that to maximize enjoyment and live longer, he must live in peace with himself and with others. He must also live in a free country."

"There are many reasons for wars. They range from the imposition of religious and ideological philosophies to the dictatorship of selfish, ruthless rulers, often malignant narcissists, who impose their will against that of their people."

"We are all cosmic brothers, despite the diversity of our origin, race, and basic beliefs. As brothers, we must always help each other, not only for survival reasons, but because of the inner satisfaction gained by helping others."

"When the citizens of a country fail to exercise the right that they have to periodically change the leaders of their government, and a dictatorship is imposed upon them, all the nations of this world should agree to a mechanism that will provide for a rapid change. In so doing, this will prevent the unnecessary death and suffering of many thousands of people, many who receive merciless punishment, and many who die trying to promote a change."

"As with any disagreement, a peaceful solution is always the best. I believe there should be a Court of the World, where anyone being accused of improper conduct has a chance to defend himself and answer to the accusations of his fellow men. All the dictators should be brought to court in front of an international jury. The dictator should abide by the decision of the court. If that would be the case, dictatorships would be short-lasting."

"Until the day that such a mechanism is established, I am afraid that local and international protests, proof of the ruthlessness of the dictator, economical blockades, and other measures, may never solve the problem."

"We are fortunate to have developed weaponry that is intended for defense but can be used to punish individuals who deserve punishment when this is determined by an international organization. An ultimatum should be given to every dictator. If he or she is unwilling to yield the control of their country, they must be removed without the sacrifice of innocent people. We have a saying in Spanish, "Thieves who steal from thieves, deserve 100 years of pardon." This dictatorship ended in the hands of vicious men. It is practical to end them as quickly as possible. May all the citizens of the world live in peace are my wishes."

CHAPTER 35

SIMON'S SURPRISE

Mixed with the crowd were three familiar faces watching and listening to Simon. They were Ivan, Quico, and Miguel. They had been rescued by a patrol boat from Isla Grande and were hungry for revenge. From a distance they watched Simon. Their expression of hatred contrasted with that of the crowd. Ivan pulled a gun and hid behind a column. He aimed his gun at Simon.

A woman and her daughter, who were walking towards the crowd, observed the three men who had guns in their hands and were aiming them at Simon and Tony. They screamed, then struck the gunmen with their hands and purses. Suddenly the sound of a bullet was heard.

Simon and Tony ducked and then glanced in the direction from which the gun had been fired. They immediately recognized their hated enemies. Ivan, Quico, and Miguel shot again but the crowd surrounded them, forcing them to run out of the Airport. Simon and Tony joined the police force in their chase. A policeman shot and hit Miguel in his right thigh. He fell and was easily captured. Ivan and Quico ran towards the parking garage. Simon took Miguel's gun and Tony was armed by a security guard.

Ivan and Quico ran into the parking garage, followed closely by Simon and Tony. Police cars reached the scene. Ivan and Quico ran up the ramp looking for their car. As they saw policemen coming down the ramp, and Simon and Tony coming up, they decided to use the stairs. They rushed to the roof of the Airport parking garage, followed by Simon and Tony. They turned and shot down the stairwell, trying to hit Simon and Tony, who were able to avoid the bullets. Ivan and Quico reached the roof. Simon and Tony arrived a few seconds later. They started shooting at each other. Tony fatally wounded Quico. Ivan crouched behind air conditioning equipment and shot his last bullet, which missed Simon. When he tried again to shoot, his gun merely clicked, empty.

When Simon realized that Ivan had no more bullets, he threw away his gun and ran towards Ivan. There was an intense fistfight. At one point Simon was forced over the wall and Ivan tried to push him onto the street. Simon looked down from the roof of the seven story building, and in a desperate move, hit Ivan in the stomach, pushing him with his feet; Ivan flew over him and landed on the pavement of the parking garage with a sickening thud. Simon and Tony's enemies had met their well-deserved destiny.

Simon joined his brother, Tony. They embraced and walked closely together out of the building. There was a beautiful sunset and another crowd greeted them. This was finally the end of their ordeal.

CHAPTER 36

The sun was setting in the Florida Keys. Ramon had completed his narration of The Omega Project.

Ramon then said to Annie, "Your parents settled in Miami and, after a few months, your grandmother and I came from Isla Grande. Alex was of great help in bringing us to the United States. We were all lucky to find jobs and prospered financially. I have been given the opportunity to buy this boat which I use to cruise with the family and go fishing."

"May the Lord protect innocent people around the world from ruthless dictators. Let's enjoy the rest of the day."

With these words, they proceeded cruising slowly towards Miami.

Annie and Johnny never forgot Ramon's story. The vision of an empty vessel and the thoughts of what may have happened to its occupants lived in their minds for the rest of their lives.

E N D

A STATEMENT
FROM BYRON DARING

"I do not pretend to be a spokesman for any exiles but I do believe that I can voice the feeling of a majority of grateful people in exile. I would hope that they share with me this prayer:

"Thanks, O God, for allowing us to live in times of great developments in countries where there is freedom, democracy, and prosperity. Thanks for giving us the health that enables us to enjoy, learn, work, and help our fellow men. Thanks to you and to the United States of America, and other countries of the world for receiving, welcoming, and helping exiles and for giving them the opportunity of rebuilding their lives by working and living, peacefully, freely, and with dignity. Give us, O Lord, the energy to help everyone, everyday."

"No country has done so much for so many as the United States of America, and, particularly for the exiles of unfortunate nations, close and far away. No other nation has received such a massive number of immigrants, from almost every country in the world, giving them the opportunity to live in peace, with dignity and freedom. My wishes are that fundamental changes take place in any country ruled by a dictatorship. I deeply hope that democracy in those countries will provide for adequate living standards and the restoration of human rights."

ABOUT THE AUTHOR

Byron Daring is the pseudonym of a young, imaginative author of numerous science-fiction books. Although his true name is not revealed, he has been a philosopher, a teacher of humanities, and a good friend of those who suffer. He has lived and traveled extensively throughout Europe, Africa, Asia, and America; however, his current whereabouts are unknown. He has used his vast knowledge and his contacts with friends from exile to write this novel. Readers of this book should think about the suffering of those who live under oppressive regimes. We can always administer assistance to those in need, regardless of where we are, and to whom the help is directed. We have an obligation to give back something of what we receive and that is one thing we should always keep in mind.